BEWARE!!
DO NOT READ THIS
BOOK FROM
BEGINNING TO END!

It's back!

And it wants you . . .

Your aunt and uncle have a surprise. They're taking you to a carnival. But once you get there, you realize it's the Carnival of Horrors! Noooooooo!

"Play or pay," says Big Al, the evil carnival manager. You have till midnight to find the ride that will get you out. Or you can try to beat Big Al at his own games.

So, choose: fight squid and ride the Roller Ghoster, or test your game skills at the most sinister arcade ever. One thing is for sure — you'd better hurry. . . .

You are in control of this scary adventure. You decide what will happen.

Start on PAGE 1. Then follow the instructions at the bottom of each page. You make the choices. Choose wisely.

And now, take a long, deep breath. Cross your fingers. And turn to PAGE 1 to *GIVE YOUR-SELF GOOSEBUMPS!*

READER BEWARE —
YOU CHOOSE THE SCARE!

Look for more
GIVE YOURSELF GOOSEBUMPS adventures
from R.L. STINE

R.L. STINE

GIVE YOURSELF

Goosebumps®

RETURN TO THE CARNIVAL
OF HORRORS

AN
APPLE
PAPERBACK

SCHOLASTIC INC.
New York Toronto London Auckland
Svdnev New Delhi Hong Kong

A PARACHUTE PRESS BOOK

ISBN-13: 978-0-590-21062-1

This edition is for sale in Indian subcontinent only.

First Scholastic Printing, December 1996
Reprinted by Scholastic India Pvt. Ltd., January; March 2008;
January; August 2010; November 2011; January 2012;
July; October 2013; August; December 2014; July; October 2015

Printed at Shivam Offset Press, New Delhi.

"AAAAAAAAGH!" you scream. You sit straight up in bed. The room is pitch-black. Your heart pounds in terror.

You take a shaky breath. It was only a bad dream, you tell yourself. The same bad dream you always have. About the Carnival of Horrors.

That terrifying carnival came to your town last summer. But instead of taking the usual rides and playing the same hokey games, you had to fight for your *life*! Somehow, you escaped.

You sigh and lie back down. Your eyes begin to adjust to the darkness.

Hey. Wait.

This isn't your room!

Turn to PAGE 2.

You open your mouth to scream again. Then you realize where you are. You're in your bedroom on your aunt and uncle's farm. They invited you and a friend for a visit.

Your door opens, and your friend Patty steps into the room. "You woke me up," she complains. "I don't know which is worse, you or that dopey, noisy rooster." She peers at your sweaty face and the rumpled sheets on your bed. "Dreaming about the Carnival of Horrors again?"

You nod. Patty was trapped at the carnival with you.

"You guys are awake?" Your cousin Floyd pokes his head into your room. "Amazing. You're never up this early."

Floyd is a year younger than you and Patty. But he towers over you both. He's really skinny and wears thick glasses. He's a computer whiz but also a total klutz.

"Want to help me milk the cows?" he asks.

Poor cows. Floyd will probably trip and knock them over.

"We have to get dressed," you tell him. You sniff the air. *Mmmmmm*. Pancakes! "And eat!"

"Good morning!" Aunt El greets you when you get downstairs. She brings a platter of pancakes to the table. "We have a big surprise for you kids!" she announces.

Find out what it is on PAGE 3.

"A surprise?" Patty says.

"Is there a new movie?" you ask. The local theater has only one dinky screen. It's been showing the same gooey love story for weeks.

"Better than that!" Aunt El says. "A carnival has come to town!"

A *carnival*? You choke on your pancake. "You guys go without me. I think I'm coming down with, um, whooping cough." You cough a few times.

They're not buying it.

"Nonsense!" Uncle Steve declares. "You don't want to miss a treat like this!"

But you *do* want to miss it! After the Carnival of Horrors, you never want to see another carnival again!

You turn to Patty for help.

No luck.

"Great!" she cheers. "Can we go tonight?"

You give her a stunned look. "Lighten up," she whispers to you. "It won't be *that* carnival. It will be fun!"

You can't argue your way out of it. By evening, you're all in your uncle's pickup truck, driving to the carnival.

Turn to PAGE 4.

4

"Hop out here, kids," Uncle Steve says. He pulls up to the large colorful arches that mark the entrance to the carnival. "We'll park and meet you at the cotton-candy stand."

You, Floyd, and Patty scramble out of the pickup. You gaze at the huge carnival in front of you. It's bigger than some shopping malls you've seen.

A roller coaster towers above the fairgrounds. Giant mechanical dinosaurs swing their heads back and forth over the high surrounding fence. "Cool," you murmur in spite of your fear.

"Come on!" Patty cries. She and Floyd charge through the entrance. You follow more slowly, still feeling nervous.

Relax, you tell yourself. Carnivals are fun, remember?

You step through the entrance. You hear whistles and bleeps coming from the midway. It must be at least three blocks long, lined by booths filled with flashing video games.

At first, the blinking lights and blaring music dazzle you. Then you realize the booths look familiar.

So does the castle looming ahead of you. And the haunted house perched on the hill.

Oh, no!

"We've got to get out of here!" you gasp. "This is the Carnival of Horrors! It's back!"

Turn to PAGE 5.

"Get out of here?" Floyd repeats. "We just walked in!"

"You don't understand!" you wail. "This is the Carnival of Horrors. It's run by terrible creatures. They try to trap people here forever!"

Patty glances around. You watch the color drain from her face. "This *is* the Carnival of Horrors," she whispers. "Uh-oh. We're in big trouble."

Floyd glares at you and then at Patty. "Quit trying to scare me," he complains. "It's not funny."

"Believe me, this is no joke," you tell him. "And if we don't find a way out of here fast, we may wind up as carnival prisoners ourselves."

Floyd gazes at you a moment. You can tell he doesn't believe you. Then he shrugs. "Fine. Let's say this is some kind of monster carnival. What do we do now?"

"Maybe they haven't noticed us yet," you say. "We could mix in with the crowd on the midway and sneak back out."

"But last time, we used the rides to escape," Patty argues.

If you go to the midway, turn to PAGE 59.
If you head for the rides, turn to PAGE 122.

You kick hard, trying desperately to keep from going under. This is so weird, you think. I'm usually a good swimmer.

And what's with this life preserver? you wonder. It feels very heavy. Instead of helping you float, the life preserver seems to be dragging you down.

You bring it up to your face. You peer closely at it. Why is the orange coating chipping away?

Because it's metal underneath! You're using a life preserver made of lead.

And you know what that means.

You're sunk!

THE END

In spite of your warning, Floyd reaches for the ticket. He grabs it and yelps in pain.

You and Floyd stare at each other as you both realize the awful truth. You've both injured your video-game-playing hands!

"What rotten luck," Big Al purrs. "Well, there's still one member of your team who can play. And as it says right there" — he points to the ticket on the ground — "I get to choose the game. And I choose Super-Fiend. I'm the carnival champ!"

You have no choice. Patty starts playing. She tries her best at the unfamiliar game, but — well, you know the score.

Big Al's booming laughter sends shivers up your spine. "Hah!" he guffaws. "If you can turn *this* lousy score into a win, I'll stand on my head and let everybody go!"

The boy in the cap steps up. "Excuse me." He plucks the photograph from your pocket. Furious, you snatch it back from him.

You crumple the photo in your good hand. It curls around, showing Big Al standing on his head. You drop the picture to the ground as you desperately try to think of some way to save yourself and your friends!

If you argue with Big Al, turn to PAGE 71.
If something else occurs to you, turn to PAGE 47.

Wind howls in your face as the Roller Ghoster goes through some hair-raising curves and down a steep hill. Patty and Floyd are screaming. But all the time, you peer ahead to the Hall of the Mountain King. You have to calculate the exact second to put your plan into action.

The roller coaster climbs very high, then roars along a slope that seems to point straight down. You want to cover your eyes. But you can't. You've got to keep looking for your chance.

Now the tracks rise higher and higher, heading into a curve to the left.

Oh, no! There's a twenty-foot gap between one section of the curved track and the rest.

"Dead Man's Curve," a ghostly voice croons behind you. "Our favorite part of the ride."

Turn to PAGE 107.

Unfortunately, the squidlet you removed falls onto your other leg. It wraps its free tentacles around your ankles.

It's just as if someone tied your shoelaces together.

SPLOSH! You fall facedown in the water.

As you try to get back to your feet, more baby squid swarm over you.

There are just too many of them. There's no way to tie all those flailing tentacles together. You splash around in the water, sinking deeper. The yells of the crowd fade away.

No doubt about it, the squid have definitely won this match. Hands down. Or tentacles down. And for that, you have to hand it to them. Or, tentacle it —

Oh, never mind. Just face it. This is

THE END.

The three-eyed woman removes her blindfold. You hold your breath. Will she guess the symbol you landed on?

Her finger reaches out and touches . . .

That's where you landed!

Oh, no! Are you going to explode like the soldier?

You squinch up your eyes and clench your fists, waiting for the big bang. But nothing happens. Except that suddenly, you feel lighter. And a little chilly. "Guess they missed," you mutter.

Patty opens her eyes — and screams!

"What?" Floyd peeks between his fingers. And faints!

"What's wrong?" you demand. You glance down at yourself.

Your arms and legs — they're just bones! Your hands rush to your face. Bony fingertips click against your skull.

You're a skeleton!

Now you understand. The symbols determine your fate. The soldier landed on a bomb, and he blew up.

"No fair!" you cry. This wasn't a game of *skill*, it was a game of *skull* — and crossbones!

Don't feel too bad. At least you'll be a big hit on Halloween!

THE END

"As a matter-of-fact, I do have a camera," you declare. You pull out the instant camera you won earlier. The one that reminded you of that GOOSEBUMPS story *Say Cheese and Die!* "But I don't know if —"

The boy doesn't let you finish. "Great. Let's line up here." He beckons to a passing girl. "Would you mind snapping us?"

The pale-faced young woman wears a long skirt and a bonnet. But she must have used instant cameras before. She points and clicks. A moment later, a picture is developing in your palm.

You stare at the strange photo. You and Floyd aren't in it! Instead, it shows the boy in the cap shaking hands with a grinning Big Al. Patty has a horrified look on her face. Letters gleam on the signboard robot with the words:

FINAL SCORE:

Beside Big Al, the score reads: 53507
Beside Patty, it reads: 34
Before you can figure out what the picture means, a loud, hearty voice calls you. "I understand you want to play a little game," the voice booms.

Yikes! It's Big Al!

Turn to PAGE 105.

This is going to be tough, you think. "How will we know who to trust and who —"

Before you can finish your sentence, Ernie stomps away from you. "Quit bothering me, you little brats!" he yells.

"But — but —" you sputter. What's with this guy? One second he's offering to help you, and the next he's treating you like an enemy. Talk about moody!

Then you spot a big, hulking shape in the crowd. *Big Al!*

"Quit wasting time!" the carnival manager roars at you. "You're supposed to be playing our games, not annoying our other, um . . . *guests!*"

You get the message. You glance at the two nearest booths. One has a sign blinking: LUCKY DAY! LUCKY DAY! LUCKY DAY!

The other has a glowing hand that turns into a fist, and then an eye. Small lights spell out HAND-EYE CHALLENGE.

Which game? you wonder. Then you remember Ernie. It's time to put his offer to the test. Will he give you a hint?

You gaze at Ernie. He stares toward the Hand-Eye Challenge. Then his right eye slowly closes.

Was that your hint?

If you take Ernie's advice, turn to PAGE 133.
If you don't trust him, go to PAGE 27.

As you open your mouth to answer, something pops into your brain. The message from the maze — "Any Year Is A Number."

"1902 and 1997," you mutter. Hmmmmm. Both are years.

But both are also numbers!

Hey, there *is* a catch to this money test!

"Come on, kid, what's your answer?" Big Buck demands.

"1,997 dollar bills are worth more than 1,902," you declare.

"Um, eh, ah, er," Big Buck stammers.

"I just beat you, Big Buck!" You grin. "We won!"

"Don't forget your prize!" Patty pipes up.

"Prize. Right." Big Buck reaches under the counter and hands you a battered instant camera. "Here. Now beat it!"

It's not a great prize. But considering you're at the Carnival of Horrors, it could be a lot worse.

"Let me take your picture," you say to Patty and Floyd.

They pose in front of the booth. The camera flashes, and a moment later the picture slides out.

But Patty and Floyd don't smile up at you from the snapshot.

Instead, it's a picture of your friends screaming in terror as carnival creatures chase them!

Turn to PAGE 77.

"I'm with Patty," you announce. "Let's ride the Roller Ghoster."

This roller coaster seems a lot bigger than the one on your last adventure. It must take up a quarter of the fairgrounds, switching and branching. Some of its tracks wind around other attractions.

Two tracks split off to either side of the castle in the middle of the carnival. That's the Hall of the Mountain King. You squint at the section of rails that go behind the castle turrets.

Is it your imagination, or is there a gap in the track over there?

A roller coaster comes speeding along the nearer branch, distracting you. It sounds normal enough. The rattle and roar of the wheels mix with screams from the passengers.

Well, maybe there's a little too much screaming.

Go to PAGE 45.

"Sorry, but we don't have a camera with us," you explain.

"Well, then, you need one," the pale-faced boy insists. He points to some game booths nearby. "One of those games gives away cameras as a prize. You have to keep playing until you win a camera."

"But —" you try to argue.

The kid tugs on the brim of his cap and looks around. Then he gives you a fierce look — the look of someone who's telling you something he shouldn't.

"You need a camera if you're going to beat Big Al," he whispers. "Remember that — now scoot!"

You heard the kid! Scoot over to PAGE 54.

"What were you doing in the water?" the man demands. "You know this is where we keep the squid for the Squid Wrestling Extravaganza!"

Maybe you got water in your ears. You couldn't have heard him right. "Did you say squid wrestling?" you ask.

"That's right. But you shouldn't have tried to sneak in and practice," the man scolds. "That's cheating!"

"Wait a second!" you burst out. "We're not squid wrestlers!"

"Sure you are," the man insists. "Why else would you be in the tank?"

You don't know how to answer that.

Don't try! Just turn to PAGE 51.

You glance up. And nearly faint.

You're staring at a giant claw! A claw the size of a car!

The claw swoops down and grabs you. It swings you through the air and drops you into a plastic chute. You slide down the chute, screaming, into a giant glass box.

Patty and Floyd tumble after you. The three of you pick yourselves up, groaning. "What happened?" Patty demands.

Silently, Floyd points to one of the glass walls. You glance through it — and scream again.

Peering back at you is a giant face. Big Al's face! The carnival manager grins horribly. "Got you!" he mouths.

"Oh, no," Patty wails. "Look up!"

You gaze upward.

The giant claw dangles over your head. Slowly it begins to lower down toward you. Opening and closing. Opening and closing.

Now you understand the awful truth.

You're inside the claw game! *You're* one of the tiny people!

You're not sure how it happened. Maybe the strange green light shrank you. All you know is, you're in big trouble.

Your only hope is that someone will fish you out of there. Then maybe you can escape.

The problem is, nobody ever wins this game!

THE END

"Do your stuff, Floyd," you tell your cousin.

Floyd pats his pockets, then pulls out a big multiblade pocket knife. Using the screwdriver attachment, he removes the back of the signboard robot.

"WARNING! DO-NOT-TAMPER-WITH-THIS-UNIT!" the robot blares.

"Can you shut him up?" you ask. The voice is *so* annoying.

Floyd yanks a wire, and the voice cuts off. *"Hmmm,"* he mutters, fiddling inside the robot. You peer into the mass of wires.

"Something's wrong!" Patty cries. "The clock on the screen has changed."

You race around to the front of the robot. Patty is right. Single digits flash on the screen now.

9 . . . 8 . . . 7 . . .

"What did you do, Floyd?" you demand.

"Nothing!" Floyd insists. "I just cut this wire, which leads to the self-detect system —" He peers closer. "Wait. Does that say self-detect? Oh. Whoops."

"What *does* it say, Floyd?" you ask.

"Um. Well. It says self-destruct," Floyd mumbles.

Self-destruct? You stare at Patty, then at the screen.

3 . . . 2 . . . 1 . . .

THE EN-*KABOOM!*

"I don't care if you think I'm a wimp," you tell Patty. "I'm not getting on that roller coaster."

You walk away from the man with the cigar and the horn. "I'm trying the Slug Subway," you call over your shoulder.

The person in charge of the Slug Subway is a smiling elderly woman with puke-green skin. "Oh, you'll enjoy this ride," she gushes.

She shows you the Slug Subway. It's a long tunnel, lined with what looks like a gray carpet. But it's not a rug. The floor is covered with oozing, slimy slugs!

"Too bad we don't have any salt," Patty mutters. "We could dissolve all those creepy-crawlies."

The grandmotherly woman gasps. "My dear, these are pets, carefully trained. Watch!" She steps onto the carpet of slugs. She glides out for a couple of yards, then glides back.

She doesn't move her feet — the slugs move her!

"They must be strong," you say.

"Oh, they are strong," the old woman says, beaming. "In more ways than one!"

Go to PAGE 135.

The Roller Ghoster picks up speed. It climbs, high, higher — and then zooms down.

So far, that's pretty much like any roller coaster. But now you have a new reason to scream as you go rushing down. Screws and bolts are popping out of the wooden supports!

Up ahead, you spot another branch-off point. A small sign points to the right. It says PIT STOP.

But the ghostly chorus begins chanting again, "Left, left. Go left!"

"Don't listen to them!" Patty screams. "They want us to die, the way they did. They'll steer us to our doom!"

"Un-unless they're trying to fake us out," Floyd stammers. "Maybe they're yelling 'Go left' because they really want us to go *right*!"

"Don't be a jerk, Floyd!" Patty snaps.

"Who are you calling a jerk?" Floyd yells.

You whip your head back and forth between your friends. They're too busy arguing to be any help.

But you have a plan. You can't help grinning as you crouch over the steering wheel.

Prepare for a sharp turn — to PAGE 46.

"Come on! We can lose them!" you yell. You head for The Sand Trap. Patty and Floyd follow right behind you.

The Sand Trap looks like a golf driving range. A few people in old-fashioned clothes stand along a big red line. They're knocking golf balls toward targets sticking out of the glittering white sand.

You, Patty, and Floyd dart past them, cutting across the sandy lot.

"Hey! Don't go in there!" one of them yells.

"You're ruining the game!" another screams.

"It's dangerous!" someone shouts.

You ignore them. You figure you have only two dangers to worry about right now: being caught by the mob chasing you, or getting conked on the head by a golf ball!

Cutting across the lot isn't as easy as you thought it would be. Running through sand is tough. And the farther out you go, the more sand you find yourself scuffing through. You sink deeper and deeper.

The sand is up to your knees.

In fact, it's *past* your knees!

Brush the sand off this page and head over to PAGE 24.

"Number two is the shorter message," you answer. "But it doesn't make much sense."

You read the message aloud. " 'Any Year Is A Number.' " You turn to Patty and Floyd. "What does *that* mean?"

Floyd raises his eyebrows and shrugs.

"Who cares what it means?" Patty responds. "As long as it's the right answer!"

"It's right, all right," the man behind the counter grumbles. More smoke gushes out of his ears. "The screen always gives good advice," he adds. He vanishes behind the booth's back curtain.

"Well, that's one game we've won," you declare. "Let's keep going!"

"Hey!" Floyd exclaims. "You won the game! Don't you get a prize?"

"Good thinking," you say. "Maybe the prize will be useful."

You dash back to the booth to claim your prize. But the glittering lights, the computer screen, the man with the smoking ears — they're all gone!

An entirely different booth stands in its place.

Scratch your head and go to PAGE 61.

"I *am* feeling lucky," you reply. After all, you've come through the last few games pretty well. And if the soldier just lost, maybe the odds are in your favor.

The three-eyed woman can't win every game, can she?

The woman presses a button, and a new Q appears. She pulls on her hood.

Pick a number between eight and fourteen. Then, starting at the ☺, count up the tail and clockwise along the Q. Then count backwards (counterclockwise) around the circle, the way the soldier did. Right before he blew up.

Remember the symbol you landed on. Now it's your three-eyed opponent's turn — on PAGE 10.

"We're sinking!" you cry.

"No kidding!" Patty snaps. "Now what do we do?"

You can't go any farther. The sand is up to your waist.

"This makes no sense," Floyd exclaims. "Quicksand is wet. This stuff is dry."

"Nothing makes sense at this crazy carnival!" you wail.

The Sand Trap is living up to its name. You are definitely trapped in the sand!

If only you had noticed the sinking golf balls! You might have made a different choice. . . .

Listen, you're such a nice kid, you're going to get a second chance. But you have to keep it quiet. And this time — pay attention!

Sneak back to PAGE 62.

With a *WHOOSH*, something swoops down from the tower.

"Bats!" Patty yells.

But, no. These creatures have wings like bats. But they have the bodies of small monkeys. They fly around you, chattering.

Patty cries out as one nips her on the finger. "Get out of here, you stupid monkey!"

"I'm no monkey," the flying creature retorts. "I'm an imp!"

"What are you doing?" another imp asks as it lands on your head.

"Trying to stay on this wall!" you snap, brushing it away with your hand.

"Temper, temper," the imp scolds. It yanks your ear.

"Ow! Cut that out!" You swat at the imp, and then pull yourself up another few feet. You hear Floyd laughing.

"What's so funny?" you demand.

"Nothing!" he screams. "They're tickling me!"

"Hang on! Keep climbing!" you cry.

Finally, in spite of the imps, you reach the tower window. You and Patty and Floyd climb through.

"No fair! We're not allowed in!" an imp whines.

"Good," you mutter. You check your watch: 11:46. "If we're going to find anything, we'd better find it fast."

Time is running out! Turn to PAGE 48.

You bump into Patty and Floyd, who are right behind you. They have no place to go. A huge crowd of the strange carnival people surround you at the Hand–Eye Challenge booth.

You shiver. The carnival people stand watching silently. It gives you the creeps. They seem very interested in the outcome of the game. You almost feel as if they're rooting for you!

"This is a test of hand–eye coordination," the young woman explains, smiling broadly. Her fangs glisten in the light of the game sign.

You try to smile back, which isn't easy. Her breath smells as if she's been eating skunk casserole.

"These are for you," she says. She holds out two long, thin daggers.

Your eyes widen. Daggers? What sort of test is this, anyway?

Find out on PAGE 68.

Wait a minute, you think. What do I really know about Ernie? After all, he *is* one of the carnival people. His hint could be a trick.

You glance at the flashing signs for Lucky Day. Everyone by that booth seems happy. They're all laughing.

"I'll go with Lucky Day!" you say.

The crowd around you parts as you head over to the booth.

You glance back. Big Al is right behind you.

Ernie has vanished.

Turn to PAGE 102.

The hot-dog man looks surprised. "You actually won?" he whispers.

"Yes, he won!" Patty insists. "And we're witnesses!"

"So where's his prize?" Floyd demands.

The hot-dog man glances around. Then he swings up part of his counter on a hinge. It makes an opening large enough for you to squeeze through. "You'll have to come back here," he explains.

You step through, but he slams the counter down before Patty and Floyd can follow. "Just you," the hot-dog man barks. "We can't let crowds through. Against the rules."

"Wait for me here," you instruct Patty and Floyd.

The hot-dog man leads you to the back of the booth. He pulls aside a canvas tent-flap. "Charlie, the Letter-Go operator, is back there," he tells you.

You peer through the opening. It's pitch-black on the other side. "I can't see!" you complain.

The hot-dog man hands you an old-fashioned lantern. "Here," he grunts. "Are you going or not?"

To claim your prize from Charlie, turn to PAGE 129.

If you don't want to go into the dark tent, turn to PAGE 82.

Big Buck waves his hands in front of your face. Green sparks fly from his fingertips.

"Your bet was off by ninety-five," he booms. "So for your prize, I'll give you back that number. In *years*!"

A red glow surrounds you. "Hey! What's going on?" you cry.

You step toward Big Buck, but it's almost more than your muscles can take. You're filled with aches and pains, and your bones creak as you move.

You put a shaky hand on the counter. Something is wrong! Your hand is like a claw! The skin is wrinkled, with big brown blotches.

Your face feels all wrinkled too. "Help!" you gasp. Your teeth feel loose — and your hair is falling out!

Patty stares at you and screams.

Floyd squints his eyes at you. "Wow! You look just like that portrait of Great-grandma Louise up in the attic," he says.

"You never should have bet that guy," Patty wails.

You clutch the counter. You feel too weak to stand up.

Will you ever escape the terrible Carnival of Horrors now?

Don't bet on it!

THE END

Ernie glances around. He motions for you to step closer. "We can give you hints — warn you away from the really dangerous games," he explains in a low voice. "Some of them are rigged. Total fakes. Others are so hard to play, you may die trying! And as you've probably noticed, losing a game here means disaster!"

"No kidding," you murmur.

"We'll try to keep you safe," Ernie finishes.

You frown. You're really disappointed. "Is that all you can offer?" you complain. "I figured you could give us hints on how to win. Or . . ."

"Or rewire the controls," Floyd pipes up.

"Or show us the exit!" Patty cries.

Ernie holds up a hand. "Hold on!" he exclaims. "We can't be too obvious. If Big Al even suspects that we're helping you —" He breaks off and shudders.

You glance at Floyd and Patty, raising your eyebrows. They just shrug.

"We'll be rooting for you," Ernie adds. "Well, those of us who can still think straight, anyway."

Go on to PAGE 12.

You land on the top of the castle wall. Patty lands beside you. Floyd comes up short. His fingers clutch at a stone block, slipping. But you and Patty each grab an arm and haul him to safety.

You watch, horrified, as the Roller Ghoster rattles to the gap in Dead Man's Curve. It teeters, then crashes to the ground.

Your eyes are wide as you gaze at the wrecked Roller Ghoster. "Th-th-that could have been us!" you stammer.

"This is no time to freak out!" Patty cries.

Time? You glance at your watch. There's less than half an hour until midnight!

"We're almost out of time," you say. "Should we search the castle and try to find some way to get back the time we lost? Or" — you peer down at the rides below — "do we search for the ride that will get us out of here?"

Which will you do?

To search the castle, turn to PAGE 125.
If you head back down to the rides, try PAGE 57.

Your log rushes along a concrete channel. The sides veer in to funnel you toward the buzz saw. And they're already higher than your head. You can't just jump off!

You have an idea! You reach under the seat and yank out a big orange life preserver. Leaning forward, you stuff it down the side of the boat, between the log and the concrete wall.

It works! The tight fit makes the boat jam in place. It comes to a screeching stop.

You don't waste time. You and your friends unsnap yourselves and scramble over the top of the concrete wall.

You just make it ashore as the next log in line slams into your old boat. It hurtles forward. The buzz saw slices the log neatly in two. You gasp as the bright orange preserver gets caught on the blade, swinging round and round.

"It really was a life preserver," you tell Patty with a grin.

"Right," she replies. Then she glances around. "You know, we're back behind the scenes here, where most people can't go. Let's search the place and see what we can find!"

Search for PAGE 121 first.

A new spotlight comes on, blazing down on a metal chute set in the wall over your head.

"And now," the announcer's voice rises in excitement, "let's get ready to RUM-BLE!"

The sound coming from the chute isn't exactly a rumble. It's more like a gurgle.

A waterfall gushes out — along with dozens and dozens of baby squid!

One lands on your arm and wraps its tentacles around it.

CHOMP! It takes a bite out of you.

Yeow! There's nothing small about the size of the pain!

Hurry to PAGE 50.

34

You jump when a hand lands on your shoulder. "Don't waste your time talking to Clem. He's stuck back in the last century."

You gaze at the man who is speaking. With his odd hat and overcoat, he looks like he stepped out of an old black-and-white gangster movie.

"My name's Ernie," the man introduces himself. "I've been trapped here fifty years. But this carnival has been catching people for *centuries*."

Ernie glances around. "We all took Big Al's Challenge," he tells you. "And we all lost. But there's a legend among us carnival prisoners." Ernie lowers his voice. "If someone escapes the carnival *twice*, we will all go free!"

He stares at you and Patty, a fierce light shining in his dark eyes. "You escaped from Big Al once. Can you do it again?"

"We're sure trying," Patty replies.

Ernie nods. "Good. We'll do what we can to help you. I'll spread the word."

This is great news — isn't it?

If you trust Ernie and his carnival pals, turn to PAGE 70.

If you don't, turn to PAGE 118.

As soon as you're all strapped in, the mechanical Tyrannosaurus rex shuts its mouth and stands up. It starts walking. You can see where it's going because there are portholes where the dinosaur's eyes should be.

"Cool!" you exclaim. You're riding eighteen feet up in the air while giant legs stomp on the earth below you.

"Do you think we're going back in time?" Patty asks.

You glance out the dinosaur's windows. Everything looks exactly the same. "I don't think so," you admit.

"How about an exit? Can you see one?" Floyd asks.

"No." You start feeling discouraged. "Maybe we should check out this mechanical beast. Find the way to make it take us back in time."

Patty twists around in her seat. She nods toward a metal panel. "Maybe that's something useful," she suggests.

You stretch against your safety strap and peer at the sign on the panel: DO NOT OPEN.

"It seems like a good place to start," you say.

Turn to PAGE 64.

You glare at the crowd. Then you hear the rumble of thunder. You glance up. Clouds are gathering over the Carnival of Horrors.

Maybe this is the break you've been waiting for! "Looks like this carnival is about to close on account of rain," you tell the woman with the fangs.

The carnival people leave a big circle around you and your friends. You clutch the daggers tightly and work your way through the crowd. You hear another crash of thunder.

That's when the bolt of lightning hits you.

About a jillion volts of electricity strike the knife in your left hand and go right through you. You stagger around, smelling smoke. But you're still standing.

You slap out a burning spot on your T-shirt. "Come on," you urge Floyd and Patty. "Lightning never strikes twice —"

Another lightning bolt lands — this time on the knife in your right hand. Bolt after bolt of lightning hits, until bright blue sparks fly between your two knives.

You can't tear your eyes off the dancing sparks. They seem to form six letters. . . .

THE END

"I-THOUGHT-YOU-WANTED-TO-KNOW-THE-AMOUNT-OF-TIME-YOU-HAD-REMAINING," the robot responds.

You stare at the display of numbers.

"Less than an hour to midnight!" Patty gulps.

Floyd checks his watch. "That's right."

"And if we haven't escaped by then..." You trail off.

Two ideas come to you. One is to figure out a way to use the robot to help you escape.

The other is to forget about playing these creepy games, go straight to Big Al, and challenge him to the grand finale. Why keep wasting time?

But you can't decide. You tell Floyd and Patty your ideas.

"Go for it! Straight for Big Al!" Patty cries.

Figures, you think. Patty never seems to be afraid of anything.

Your cousin the computer whiz smiles. "I bet I could tap into the robot's memory banks and find a way out!" Floyd declares.

So, which plan will you go with?

Will you reroute the robot's circuits? Turn to PAGE 18.

Will you battle Big Al? Turn to PAGE 60.

"So are you going to bring us to Big Al?" you demand.

The kid seems lost in thought. Finally, he nods. "Okay, I'll help you find Big Al. But I'd like a favor, first. Can we take a picture of all of us together?"

"Will you show up in a photo?" Cousin Floyd inquires.

"I'm not a vampire," the boy snaps. "I'm a ghoul."

Floyd shrugs. "Sorry," he mumbles.

"What do you want with a picture?" you ask.

"For good luck," the kid replies. "And this way, if things don't work out, I'll have something to remember you by."

Great, you think. A ghoul with a scrapbook. "So where can we have our picture taken?"

"Don't you have a camera?" the boy demands.

If you won a camera along the way, turn to PAGE 11.

If you need a camera, turn to PAGE 15.

You give up trying to reason with the man in the boat. He's obviously convinced you three are squid wrestlers!

Well, you might as well make the best of a bad situation. "We'll go for the small squid!" you shout after the man in the boat.

"The smaller, the better!" Patty yells.

"Teeny-tiny, itty-bitty, eensie-weensie," Floyd adds. "Please!"

"Let's try to get to shore before the squid show up," you whisper to your friends as the boatman rows away.

The three of you wade quickly along the sunken dock until the water is only up to your knees. Then you step onto concrete.

"We must be close now!" you cry.

Suddenly four things happen.

First, blinding spotlights pop on, glaring down on you. You seem to be standing in the bottom of a concrete bowl, with row after row of spectators sitting above you.

Second, a glass wall rises behind you and your friends.

Third, water is pumped in until it's up to your chest again!

And fourth, an announcement blares over your head. "Lay-deez and gentle-things! Introducing the contenders!"

Go to PAGE 104.

The ghostly head dives at your left hand with its teeth bared.

"Aaaagh!" you yell. It's going to bite you!

You jerk your hand down, out of the way.

And the wheel spins left.

Oh, no! That wasn't what you planned to do!

The hideous head roars with laughter. "Got you!" it howls.

The Roller Ghoster hurtles on. Then it starts to slow down. Then it stops completely!

A recorded announcement blares over the loudspeakers. "Due to mechanical difficulties, the Roller Ghoster will be out of service for a few minutes. Please remain seated. Keep your hands inside the ride at all times."

"Now's our chance," you whisper. You and your friends fling back the safety bar and begin climbing down. The ghostly riders shout and hiss at you. But no heads come flying your way!

You all have scrapes and splinters by the time you reach the ground. But you made it.

"Well?" Floyd says. "*Now* can we go on the Log Zoom?"

Turn to PAGE 92.

"Out! Quick! Or we're sliced and diced!" you scream.

Patty and Cousin Floyd unsnap their seat belts and leap to their feet. The log-boat begins to rock wildly.

Just before you jump out of the boat, you remember something.

The life preservers!

You reach under the seat. You grab a couple of life preservers. Then you scramble over the side.

You hold the life preservers and push one in Floyd's direction. "Here," you gasp as you tread water. You're having trouble keeping your head above the water.

Quick! Dog-paddle over to PAGE 6!

"SQUID! SQUID! SQUID!" the crowd screams.

Fine, you think. If they love the squid so much, why not give them some?

Four of the cold-blooded babies crawl all over you. When a fifth comes along, you grab it by the tentacles, swing it over your head, and hurl it into the stands.

Patty and Floyd follow your example. Soon, the chanting turns into yells and screams as the spectators begin fighting with the hungry squidlets.

"You're breaking the rules!" the invisible announcer scolds.

"What do you mean? They asked for squid, so I gave them squid," you yell. "It's the polite thing to do!"

Peeling the last squid baby off your leg, you hurl it into the stands.

Then you jump up and hook an arm over the railing in front of the first row of seats.

You're out of there! Go to PAGE 110.

"Incorrect, wrong, error, mistake, blunder, flawed answer, miscalculation!" the tinny computer voice squawks.

"Okay, okay," you mumble.

"So that you will always remember the effect of gravity, Earthling, we will show you the difference," the voice announces.

WHOOSH! Thick mist spurts out of the floor. You glance down. The shining disk you stand on isn't silver anymore. It glows a gross yellowish-brown — like the pictures of Jupiter you've seen. Suddenly, it feels as if someone is sitting on your shoulders.

Actually, it feels as if more than one person is sitting on you.

More like two people. *Giants,* you figure. And one is holding a baby.

If you can lift your finger, turn to PAGE 52.

You feel a little annoyed at Floyd's warning.

"I can handle this game!" you declare. You'll show Floyd he's not the only one who's good at video and computer games!

You take your place in front of the steering wheel built into the counter. "Let's go!" you cry.

The screen fills with cars. *VROOOOM!* They all take off.

Except yours.

"The gas!" Floyd yells. "There's a pedal on the ground!"

But there are *two* pedals. You stomp on the left one.

Oh, no! It's the brake! By the time you get your car going, you're trailing far behind the others.

You've got to catch up! You send your car screaming through turns. You pass a red car. *Yes!* Your car skids out as you career around a blue car. But you regain control. *Yes!*

The finish line appears on the screen. You fix your eyes on it. You press hard on the gas. Can you win?

But you can't make up for your slow start. A yellow car plows across the finish line.

It's over. Letters appear on the screen: YOU LOSE!

You hear wind beginning to howl overhead.

Uh-oh! Hurry over to PAGE 126!

Following the tracks, you reach the ticket booth for the Roller Ghoster. There's no line.

You're not all that surprised.

A man steps out of the booth. "What luck! You get a free ride!" He has a big belly, and a cigar sticks out the side of his mouth. He almost looks like a typical carnival worker — except for the single horn growing out of his forehead.

He smiles, showing pointed teeth, as he leads you to a silver car waiting on the tracks. It's tiny. There are only three seats across. It looks pretty flimsy to you.

"Is that thing safe?" you ask.

The roller-coaster man shrugs. "I've never had anybody come back to complain."

Why doesn't that make you feel better?

"Listen, guys," you mutter to Patty and Floyd. "Maybe this is a bad idea. Maybe we should go on — um, um" — you look around for another sign — "the Siug Subway!"

"Yeah, that sounds *really* great," Patty mocks. "Just get into the roller-coaster car. You can't wimp out now!"

Do you board the Roller Ghoster? Turn to PAGE 86.

Do you decide it's too dangerous? Turn to PAGE 19.

You shouldn't have grinned.

"I know what you're up to!" one of the ghostly passengers bellows. "You will not turn right. I'll make *sure* of it!"

Glancing back, you see the ghost pluck his head right off his neck. You try not to gag.

Then he throws it at you!

You manage to duck, but the head hovers right in front of your face. "Drive and die!" it whispers.

Your hands shake so hard, you can barely grip the wheel. But you have to make that right turn!

It won't be easy. Not with that ghostly face scowling at you. In fact, it comes down to luck. So, think back to when you put on your shoes this morning. Which went on first? The left shoe or the right?

If you put on your right shoe first, veer right to PAGE 95.

If it was the left shoe, turn left to PAGE 40.

As you watch the crumpled photo fall, the picture appears upside down to you.

Upside down!

"Floyd! Help me!" You run to Igor, the signboard robot, and grab its ankles. With Floyd's help, you haul the robot up so its feet are in the air. Its sign — the score — is now upside down. Instead of reading:

FINAL SCORE: 53507   34

It reads:

HE   LOSES :3ЯO϶S ꓕAИIꟻ

"What do you think you're doing?" Big Al roars.

"You said if there was any way we could turn this score into a win, you'd let everyone go," you shout. "You played Patty — a girl. Look at the sign! It says '*he* loses.' It must mean *you*!"

Picking up the photograph, you hold it under Big Al's nose — upside down. "Here you are, standing on your head. The sign says 'he loses.' Big Al loses!"

The muscles in Big Al's jaws knot, and you can hear his teeth grinding.

Then he opens his mouth — and lets out a huge, bellowing scream! The world starts to turn, to spin, to whirl. . . .

Turn, spin, whirl to PAGE 78.

48

You head for the top floor of the tower. You find Big Al's office and dash through the door.

Luckily, Big Al isn't inside. His desk is covered with screens, buttons, and dials. You read the labels aloud. " 'Ride Controls. Game Controls. Space/Time Door Controls.' "

Wow! You turn to Floyd. "Can you figure this out? Those Space and Time controls might help us!"

"I can try," Floyd says. He sits at the desk and begins pressing buttons. A humming sound fills the room. Then a glowing dot appears in the air. It grows into a large rectangle.

A doorknob appears on the right side of the rectangle.

Patty stares, astonished. "It's a door!"

Uh-oh. You hear footsteps! "Can you hurry?" you gulp. "I don't think we have much time!"

Floyd plays with the Space and Time dials. "I'm not sure I've got the numbers right for the door thingy," he murmurs.

The heavy footsteps get closer. It has to be Big Al!

"Come on!" you beg.

"Ten more seconds," Floyd mutters.

"We don't have ten seconds!" you screech.

To leap through the Space/Time Door now, turn to PAGE 94.

To wait as your cousin asks, turn to PAGE 91.

You dash through the tin spaceship into the Guess Your Weight on Jupiter booth. The booth's walls and roof are made of old-time computers with buttons and dials. A hairless alien with orange skin smiles at you from behind a control panel. "Welcome, Earthlings," it says.

"Look at that awesome makeup," Floyd says to you and Patty. "Or do you think it's a mask?"

"I-I don't know," you stutter. Here at the Carnival of Horrors, it could easily be a *real* alien.

You peer around Patty toward the entrance to the booth. At least none of the carnival people are following you.

The alien recites what sounds like a memorized speech. "Jupiter is the largest planet in our solar system. It has many moons."

The computer screens lining the walls flash pictures of the planet Jupiter.

"Jupiter is much, much larger than the planet Earth," the alien continues. "That means there is more than twice as much gravity."

Turn to PAGE 75.

You fling your arm around, trying to throw off the baby squid. It hangs on with its toothed tongue.

"MMMFF!" Floyd grunts. A little squid has landed on his head. Its tentacles wrap around Floyd's jaw, clamping his mouth shut. It's using another set of tentacles to choke him!

You wade over to try to help your cousin. But you stagger in midstep. Three more squid have grabbed your legs!

"What gives?" you yell at the invisible referee. "We asked for a small opponent!"

"And that's what we gave you!" the announcer answers. "You wrestle your combined weight in squid. So we gave you two hundred fifty pounds' worth. Of the small size."

"Hey, look!" Patty cries. She holds up a squirming pair of squid. "I tied two of them together!"

Maybe that's the solution! Tie all the tentacles together.

"SQUID! SQUID! SQUID! SQUID!" the crowd cries.

No one seems to be cheering for you humans anymore. You flush with anger. You feel like throwing the squid at the audience.

Hey — maybe that would work!

Should you tie the squid together? Turn to
PAGE 124.

Or should you throw the squid at the crowd?
Turn to PAGE 42.

You feel the boat bump up against an under-water dock. "Here we are!" the man announces cheerfully.

You, Floyd, and Patty scramble out of the boat — and splash down in water up to your armpits!

"Hey! Couldn't you take us closer to shore?" you ask.

"Oh, no! I might scratch the bottom of the boat. Besides, this is the best place for the next wrestling match!"

"Who'd be crazy enough to wrestle a squid?" Patty wonders.

"Why, *you* three!" replies the rapidly retreating man. "Which kind do you want, small or jumbo?"

"Hey! Wait! Don't leave us here!" Floyd begs.

"You web-footed goofball!" Patty hollers.

Your mouth hangs open as you stare after the rowboat, trying to figure out what to do.

If you want to try to convince the man you're not squid wrestlers, turn to PAGE 113.

If you give up and ask for a small-sized opponent, turn to PAGE 39.

"Hunhh!" you grunt. The breath whooshes out of you as you crumple to the ground. The circle under you glows brighter. The mist grows thicker.

You feel as if a steamroller is slowly chugging over you. Your bones creak. There's no way you can push yourself up — your arms and legs weigh too much to move.

The disk beneath you begins to hum.

"This is your correct weight on Jupiter," the voice declares.

Instead of easing up, the invisible force presses down even harder. It's crushing you!

Quick! Close this book!

SQUASH!

Too late! You're flat as a piece of paper. Flat as your little sister's singing. Flatter than Aunt El's pancakes!

In nothing flat!

THE END

"We won some games," you remind Patty and Floyd, "but we haven't escaped yet." And time is running out, you add silently.

You notice a large flashing sign up ahead. It looks like a giant letter "Q."

"Let's try that one," you suggest.

The three of you wander closer. This game is called Q Quest. You watch a man in a Civil War uniform play the game.

The player peers at a board. On it, different symbols form the letter "Q." A woman sits beside the board, blindfolded by a hood.

"Pick a number between six and sixteen," the woman instructs the soldier.

"Got it," the soldier declares.

"Now, count that many spaces along the Q. Start at the tail and go clockwise. Then count back again counterclockwise, but keep going around the Q, not back down the tail. If I guess the symbol you land on, I win."

You watch the soldier count fourteen symbols, then count back.

Go to PAGE 136.

"The sooner we start playing, the sooner we're out of here," you declare.

"Or the sooner we're doomed," Floyd moans.

You wish he hadn't said that.

A nearby booth lets out a piercing squawk. "Let's check out that one," you decide quickly.

You, Floyd, and Patty scurry over to the booth. It has an enormous computer screen hanging across the back wall.

"What's the game?" Patty asks.

"See for yourself," the man behind the counter replies.

He almost looks normal. Except for the brownish smoke coming out of his ears.

The screen flashes. A sign appears.

LETTER-GO!
BEAT THE MAZE BY FINDING THE MESSAGE!

You're pretty good at mazes and word puzzles. "I think I'll try this one," you tell Patty and Floyd.

Step right up and let 'er rip on PAGE 108.

All of a sudden, you're not thirsty anymore. You toss the soda can into a trash barrel. "I guess we'd better try another game."

You, Patty, and Floyd walk along the row of booths. "Let's see what this one is," you suggest, coming to a stop in front of a computer race-car game.

A tiny old woman rests her parasol against the counter and grabs one of the steering wheels. "These newfangled contraptions," she complains as her car falls behind. "We didn't even have horseless carriages in my day."

She comes in last. Big letters appear on the computer screen: YOU LOSE!

Your mouth drops open as a little tornado of blue light starts spinning over her head.

The woman shrieks as the tornado grows larger. Soon it engulfs her completely.

When the light-storm fades, the old woman is gone!

Turn to PAGE 93.

"So, kid," Big Buck calls to you. "Will you bet me?"

"You bet I will!" you announce. "1902 dollars are worth much more than today's money."

"Hah! You lose!" the little man cackles.

"My cousin has books —" you begin.

"I've got the proof right here," Big Buck cuts you off, waving his two stacks of bills under your nose.

He counts the bills on the counter. "There are 1,902 dollars in this pile." The man smiles at you.

You shiver. His smile isn't very friendly. "And in that pile?" you say, gulping.

"1,997 smackers," Big Buck replies, his smile growing wider. "1,997 dollars are worth more than 1,902 of them. Ninety-five bucks more, to be exact."

"No fair!" you complain. "That was a trick question!"

"Not if you know the answer!" Big Buck replies. "But to prove what a nice guy I am, I'll give you a prize, anyway."

Claim your prize on PAGE 29.

"Let's find that ride!" you exclaim. "Our ride to freedom!"

Peering down from the castle, you see tons of rides you haven't tried.

Cousin Floyd counts them off. "There's the Kaboomper Kars, the Log Zoom, the Slug Subway, the Body Buster, the Vomit Vortex —"

"Plus the merry-go-round and the kiddie rides," Patty adds.

"Let's move it!" you yell. You jump down from the wall and into the castle courtyard. You charge toward the gate.

The three of you race through it and dart down the trail to the rides.

So many rides, you think. So little time!

Thick shrubs line the path, making it hard to see. You zoom around a bend. There's something up ahead of you . . . something red and green.

Could it be? Yes! Standing on the path is a group of elves. You recognize their red pointed hats, their green outfits, and their little pointed beards. But if they are the same elves you met the last time you were at the carnival, they aren't the friendly kind.

Gulp. You can't help noticing their large, sharp axes.

Act brave! Turn to PAGE 116.

"Close enough, Earthling," says a computer voice.

You step off the silver disk. "You — you mean I win?" you sputter.

"Yes," the voice answers grumpily. "Now go."

You laugh. If a computer could make faces, this one would definitely be scowling, you think.

You leave the weighing room, feeling relieved. Patty and Floyd rush over to you.

"How did it go?" Patty asks.

"I won," you tell them. "Now let's get out of here."

You peek between the fins of the fake rocket ship.

More good news! The crowd is gone!

"We lost them!" Patty exclaims.

The three of you set off down the midway.

Hmmm, you think, I've won all the games I've played so far. How many more do I have to win to get us out of here?

If you've won enough games to challenge Big Al, turn to PAGE 137.

If not, keep playing by turning to PAGE 53.

"Forget the rides!" you tell Patty. "Let's get lost in the crowd on the midway and sneak out now!"

Patty and Floyd nod in agreement.

Darting through the crowd, you hear the *WHOOSH* of the rides, and *BINKS* and *BLOOPS* from the midway games. But why don't you hear happy yells from the kids? Or laughter from the parents?

You peer at the people around you. They all wear strange clothes, as if they were from another time.

They *are* from different times! you realize. You stare as a girl in a Pilgrim outfit strolls by with a man in clanking armor. You shudder as you notice their deathly pale faces. Their dark eyes are blank. They look . . . *dead.*

Oh, no! You recognize these people from your last visit to the carnival. They're the ghostly inhabitants of the Carnival of Horrors!

A big man in a bright checkered jacket suddenly blocks your way. His coal-black eyes glitter over a large, drooping mustache.

You gasp in horror. It's Big Al, the manager of the carnival.

Your enemy!

"Welcome back!" he cackles.

Turn to PAGE 85.

You set off down the midway, searching for Big Al. It should be easy to spot a huge guy in a tacky checkered jacket.

But now that you *want* to find him, there's no trace of the carnival manager.

What can you do?

You turn to the robot. It's been clanking along after you and your friends on its mechanical feet.

"Do you know where we can find Big Al?" you ask.

The robot makes a piercing, staticky noise. "MY-MEMORY-BANKS-DO-NOT-HAVE-THAT-DATA," it replies.

"So who else can we ask?" you wonder out loud.

You spot a boy around your age lurking in the shadows of the tents. He's wearing knickers, suspenders, and a tweed cap.

Judging by the boy's old-fashioned clothes, you know he's one of the people trapped by Big Al. Maybe he knows where the carnival manager is.

So *what are you waiting for? Ask the kid on* PAGE 132.

"Where did —" Patty cries in surprise.

"How, h-how —" Cousin Floyd sputters.

"Easy," you reply. "This is the Carnival of Horrors. Where anything can happen. And usually does!"

You cautiously approach the new booth. Instead of flashing lights, there are just a couple of dim, dirty bulbs in each corner. Behind the counter stands a fat, bald man selling hot dogs.

"Hey," you call. "What happened to the booth that was just here?"

"This *is* the booth that was just here," the man declares. His eyes dart around as if he's afraid something may sneak up on him.

"What about Letter-Go?" Floyd asks.

The hot-dog man stares at him. "Let who go?"

"That's the name of the game that was just here," you insist. "The message maze. And I won! Don't I get a prize?"

Turn to PAGE 28.

You and your friends dash straight down the midway. But the crowd keeps chasing you.

"They're catching up," Floyd gasps.

Desperately, you glance around for someplace where you can lose the creatures. You notice some kind of golfing game on one side of the midway. Above it hangs a large sign: THE SAND TRAP.

On the other side of the midway stands a huge, cheesy-looking fake rocket. There's a door cut into the bottom of it. It's the entrance to a booth with the sign GUESS YOUR WEIGHT ON JUPITER.

You can break into the golf game and cut across the sand, or you can dart through the spaceship into the Jupiter game. Maybe you could hide in there.

Which will it be?

If you cut through The Sand Trap, turn to PAGE 21.

If you try the booth with the rocket, turn to PAGE 49.

"Don't give up! We've got to get free!" you yell to Patty and Floyd. The three of you struggle even harder.

You pull, pinch, and bite the tentacle that holds you. It loses its grip! You squirm loose and swim toward the stands.

The squid lashes a tentacle at you. You splash out of its reach. It releases Patty and Floyd as it strains to reach you.

"Hurry!" you cry. "To the stands!

Patty and Floyd swim after you. You reach shallow water near the seats. The squid seems to have given up.

"Find an exit!" you tell Patty and Floyd. But the audience is clapping so loudly, your friends can barely hear you.

You've never heard such thunderous applause. You kind of like it. You take a bow.

The applause grows even louder. You gaze into the crowd. And gasp.

The audience — it's not human! The seats are filled with rows of grinning octopuses! No wonder the applause is so loud. Each octopus is clapping with all eight of its tentacles.

You're so shocked, you fall back into the water.

Instantly the waiting squid grabs you. As it drags you underwater, you think, Oh well, that's show business!

THE END

Patty strains against her belt. She can just reach the panel. It's a struggle to get it open, but she succeeds. "There's some machinery," she reports. "And a switch. It says 'Forward' and 'Back.'"

"Set it to 'Back' and see what happens," you say. "That's got to be the way for us to make up some time."

The mechanical dinosaur lurches in midstep. Then it begins walking backwards!

"Put it to 'Forward' again!" you cry.

"I can't!" Patty shouts. "It's stuck!"

You unbuckle your safety belt and peer into the open panel. Wiping away a smear of grease, you find another control. It's marked ESCAPE HATCH.

You press it. A door in the back of the Tyrannosaurus rex's head pops open.

"Yow!" You stare down the dinosaur's back. It's like a long ski-slope, ending at a pointed tail.

A tail sticking over the carnival's fence!

"Here's a way out!" you yell, pointing.

"Yeah," Floyd gulps. "If we don't fall and break our necks!"

Slide down the tail on PAGE 97.
Stick with the ride on PAGE 79.

Big Al's cruel laughter booms out of loudspeakers on both sides of the track. "Give up, kids," he thunders. "You don't have a chance! The rides close at midnight. If you haven't found the one that sets you free, you'll become our guests — forever."

"Rats!" Floyd grumbles. "Why couldn't we pick a ride where the time goes *backwards*?"

"Well, we didn't," you snap. "But we don't have time to worry about that now. We need to get off this train — fast!"

You peer over the sides of the choo-choo. The train is now chugging along a bridge high above a lake of inky-black water.

Should you jump out here? It might save you some precious time.

Or should you wait until the train reaches dry land?

Make up your mind — time's a-wasting!

If you jump now, turn to PAGE 67.
If you wait, turn to PAGE 131.

"Yiiiiiiieeeee!" you scream. Spray gets in your eyes, but you can feel the wind in your face as your log-boat whizzes downward. It hits the water at the bottom like a cannonball, sending up jets of water all around. After its splashdown, the log bobs on the surface like a cork.

"Cool!" Patty cries.

The log is pulled along by the current, heading for a large shed that looks like a sawmill. That must be where you get off the ride.

Or maybe not, you think. The log is speeding up. It wouldn't do that if you were about to park.

You fly into the make-believe sawmill. It's pitch-dark. You can't see anything. But you hear a whirring sound.

Turn to PAGE 98.

"Jump! Now!" you scream. You have less than an hour before midnight. And with the Right Away Railroad speeding up time, who knows what the clock will say once you get across the river!

Patty and Floyd leap from their seats. You follow them over the side.

SPLASH! You hit the black lake. Cold water goes up your nose. You burst to the surface sputtering for air. Which way to shore?

A bright searchlight stabs out of the darkness.

"What are you doing in the water?" a man demands from behind the light. "Don't you know it's dangerous?"

You tread water as you watch a small boat approach. You're relieved that help has come so quickly. You, Patty, and Floyd clamber aboard.

"Wow, thanks for saving us," you say, sighing with relief.

You begin to feel nervous again when you discover the man rowing the boat has webbed hands and feet.

Gulp! Go to PAGE 16.

"What do I need these for?" You try to sound confident, but your voice cracks as you ask the question.

The woman smiles, revealing her fangs again. This time you step back to avoid her stinky breath. "All you have to do is hold the daggers out at arm's length and touch one point to the other," she explains.

Phew! That seems pretty simple.

"Of course," the young woman goes on, "you have to do it with one eye closed." Her hand goes to the scrap of green silk she wears. "You can borrow my patch if you like."

"N-no, thanks," you stammer. No way do you want to see what's under there! "I can just close one eye."

Okay, now take the test. Use long, sharp pencils instead of daggers. Hold a pencil in each hand, with the point aiming straight up. Stretch out your arms as far as they'll go on either side of you. Close one eye. Then, bending your elbows, try to touch one pencil point to the other.

It's harder than it sounds, so we'll give you three tries.

If you managed to make the points touch, turn to PAGE 90.

If you missed all three times, turn to PAGE 130.

"It's got me!" you yell, trying to peel the rubbery flesh away. The tentacle feels *squishy* — but the powerful muscles underneath are like iron. They drag you down into the water.

"It's got me too!" Patty wails.

"Help!" Floyd cries, thrashing wildly in the water.

From above, you hear wild cheers and whistling. You must be putting on quite a show!

Panic floods through you. How can you survive this wrestling match? The squid is so strong!

Should you try to break free from the squid's grip and swim toward the spectators? There must be a way out of the water near the seats.

Or should you try the squid's game? It's pulling you down under the water. Suppose you pull *it* up into the air?

Make up your mind! That tentacle is making it hard to breathe!

If you try to break free, swim over to PAGE 63.
If you try to lift the squid out of the water, turn to PAGE 81.

You take a deep breath. Maybe the carnival people aren't the most trustworthy folks in the world. But they might help you escape the Carnival of Horrors. It's worth a shot!

"Okay," you whisper. "We'll trust you. Right, guys?"

Patty and Floyd both nod.

Ernie clasps his hands. "Wonderful!" he gushes.

"We need you to get us out of here," Patty admits.

"And we need *you* if we're ever going to be free!" Ernie grabs your hand and clutches it hard. "It's been so long since any of us had hope."

"Um, fine, fine," you mumble, wrestling your hand away. This guy has some grip! "Now — what can you do to help us?"

Find out on PAGE 30.

"NO FAIR!" you yell at Big Al. "You cheated with that ticket. You cheated with the game —"

"And you lost," Big Al gloats. "So now you'll be with the Carnival of Horrors — full-time. Come with me, Igor," he tells his robot. "Help me think of a job for these kids."

"CANNOT-WALK," Igor the robot crackles. "SCREW-LOOSE."

"You're always getting screws loose," Big Al complains. Then he snaps his fingers. "I know the perfect job for you three!"

He passes a hand over the three of you. Glowing dust sprinkles down.

"Nooo!" you wail. You feel yourself shrinking! Your fingers are growing together, becoming hard and metallic. By the time the transformation is complete, you only come up to Igor's knees. And your hands — they've turned into screwdrivers! The same thing has happened to Patty and Floyd.

"Now get to work! And don't screw up!" Big Al says. He bends over, he's laughing so hard at his own dumb joke.

Igor rolls over to you for repairs.

You're only going to do this job because you're being forced to, you tell yourself. Anyone who'd do this willingly, would have to ... well, have a screw loose.

THE END

The other roller-coaster cars rumble into place behind you. *Ka-CHUNK!* They link up with your car. Then all the cars lurch forward. They begin to climb. Up ahead, you see the tracks split.

"Which way?" you ask Patty and Floyd.

"Left," Patty replies promptly.

Your cousin shrugs. "Why not?"

But from the cars behind you, whispery voices begin to chant, "Right! Right! Go right!"

You glance over your shoulder to see who's talking.

Bad move.

The other passengers look as if they've been riding too long — a couple of *years* too long. Their skin stretches over their bones like dried leather. Tufts of hair cling to their scalps. They glare at you through eyes as small and wrinkled as raisins.

Now you know why this ride is called the Roller Ghoster.

They're all ghosts!

But you can't worry about that right now.

The big question is, do you go left, as your friends want, or right, as the ghostly passengers insist?

If you agree with your friends, turn to PAGE 80.

If you go along with the ghosts, turn to PAGE 76.

You gaze around, searching for a way to escape the glare of all those unfriendly eyes.

You spot the first of the rides — a kiddie choo-choo train. *Hmmmmm.* Wasn't that train a way out of the carnival last time?

You race toward it. Yes! You glance at the letters on the front of the train. "Hop aboard," you cry. "This is the Right Way Railroad. It's how we escaped before! It leads out of here!"

You, Patty, and Floyd jump aboard. With a lurch, the train starts forward. "Only a few minutes," you assure your friends, "and this carnival is history! There's a tunnel up ahead."

But something is weird. The train is moving too slowly. And the people stroll by in quick, jerky movements. It's like watching a video on fast-forward.

Glancing at your watch, you notice the hands whizzing around.

Huh? How can time be speeding up?

You lean over and peer at the name painted on the side of the train. Oh, no! This isn't the Right Way Railroad. It's the Right *Away* Railroad.

"I get it," you groan. Riding the train makes time move more quickly. And with a midnight deadline to escape — you don't have any time to lose!

Chug over to PAGE 65.

"AAAAGH!" you yell, sitting up in bed. What a nightmare! You dreamed you were back at the Carnival of Horrors!

Floyd and Patty appear in the doorway. "We're home! We escaped from that carnival!"

You gaze around. *Yes!* You're in your bedroom at Aunt El and Uncle Steve's! It wasn't a dream — you really were at the Carnival of Horrors! But Floyd rigged it so that you went back in time, and now you're safe on the farm.

You jump out of bed and get dressed. You rush downstairs, with Patty and Floyd on your heels. Aunt El is making pancakes at the stove.

"Morning, Aunt El. Anything special going on today?" you ask.

You hold your breath, waiting for her reply. Patty and Floyd fidget next to you.

"Not really," your aunt answers.

"No — um — surprises?" Floyd says.

Aunt El shakes her head. "Nothing," she answers. "I'm afraid it will be another ordinary day."

You grin broadly at Patty and Floyd.

"Perfect!" you cry. "That's just the way we like it!"

THE END

You remember a booth like this the last time you were trapped at the carnival. But then you had to guess your weight on *Mars*.

Things are always changing at the Carnival of Horrors.

"Who will go first?" the alien asks.

"I will," you volunteer.

"Good!" The alien smiles, showing sharp purple teeth sprouting from bright-green gums.

"That doesn't look like a mask to me," Patty whispers.

"Walk through to the weighing room." The alien points one of its seven orange fingers toward a metal door between the blinking computers. You notice heavy locks on it.

All of a sudden, you're not so eager to go.

"Hey," you pipe up. "That wouldn't be some kind of spaceship to Jupiter, would it?" You know how crazy this carnival can be.

The alien makes a sound that might be a laugh. "Oh, no. It's not a spaceship at all."

For all you know, the alien is lying through its purple teeth — but whatever is in that room can't be any worse than the mob that's looking for you on the midway.

Taking a deep breath, you walk through the door.

What's in the next room? Find out on PAGE 128.

You turn the steering wheel to the right. The Roller Ghoster rumbles as it switches lines — to the right-hand branch.

"What are you doing?" Patty wails. "If you take advice from those dead guys in the back, we'll end up just like them."

"Maybe," you agree. "And then again . . . maybe not."

You know that this branch veers toward the Hall of the Mountain King. The castle with its towers is the only thing that rises higher than the Roller Ghoster tracks.

That means it's the one place where you might be able to jump off the rickety coaster.

You don't mention that to Patty, however.

If the ghostly passengers in the rest of the cars hear your plan, they might try to stop you.

Keep quiet and turn to PAGE 8.

"What's wrong?" Patty asks. "Did Floyd make a dopey face?"

Silently, you show them the picture.

"It's a trick," Floyd scoffs. "They probably told Big Buck to give it to you if you won. They're trying to psych you out."

They're doing a good job! you think. You don't know about Patty and Floyd, but you're really spooked. The picture reminds you of a GOOSE-BUMPS story you read called *Say Cheese and Die!* It was about a camera that took pictures of the future. Usually the pictures showed terrible things to come.

"Do you think you can keep winning games?" Patty frets. "How many have you won, anyway? Enough to challenge Big Al?"

"Didn't you use the rides to escape before?" Floyd asks.

You stare unhappily at the picture. Which choice will land your friends in trouble?

You wish you had someone to ask for advice. But the only others around are the weird carnival people.

If you seek advice from the carnival people, go to PAGE 114.

If you try the rides, go to PAGE 122.

If you've already won three games, turn to PAGE 127.

The Carnival of Horrors whirls around you like a top gone out of control. The midway fades away, as if its millions of lights are blinking out. Big Al seems to be shrinking as he spins. Carnival ghosts swirl around you. They all look happy.

Even in the storm of noise around you, you can hear voices cry out: "Free ... at last we're all free!"

Everything disappears in a blur as you whiz faster and faster. Then you land with a thump — right at someone's feet!

"Whoa!" a familiar voice exclaims. Uncle Steve helps you up. "That must have been some wild ride — to get you *that* dizzy!"

You glance around. You, Patty, and Floyd have plopped down at the dusty entrance of a plain, ordinary, rather shabby carnival. The Carnival of Horrors is gone — forever!

"I want to go on whatever ride you were on!" Aunt El laughs. "After we all have some cotton candy!"

"But — we —" Cousin Floyd begins.

You shush him. "Cotton candy sounds great!" you declare. "I think we're going to enjoy this carnival!"

THE END

"Let's not risk it," you decide. "We're safer in the ride."

"Even if we are going backwards," Floyd adds.

You peer out the Escape Hatch. Oh, no! Your giant creature is careening into the path of another mechanical dinosaur!

The Tyrannosaurus rex nearly does a back flip when it crashes into the mechanical triceratops. And you almost go sailing out the open hatch!

"Now I see why they have those safety belts," you croak, clinging to the door frame.

The crash must have damaged the Dino-Ride. Your Tyrannosaurus rex is still lurching around, but much more slowly. Sparks flicker up through the machinery behind the hatch.

Smoke begins to rise too.

"We have to bail out!" you yell. "Now!"

Leap to PAGE 120!

80

You spin the wheel to the left. The Roller Ghoster switches tracks. It also picks up speed.

Angry hisses come from the dried-up ghosts behind you.

"Hey!" you shout back. "Who's driving this thing, anyway?"

"Foolish child," a chilling voice answers. "We all thought we were the drivers when we boarded this roller coaster. Instead, we became passengers — forever."

You don't like the sound of that.

"No matter which way you go," the voice continues, "our fate will become *your* fate."

Stop trembling and turn to PAGE 20.

"Grab hold of a tentacle!" you command Floyd and Patty.

"Why?" Floyd asks. "I've already got a tentacle grabbing hold of me!"

"Just get a good grip — and heave!" you yell.

You feel as if you're playing a watery game of tug-of-war. But your steady pressure finally wins. The body of the squid rises out of the water. It looks squishy, like a sack of grayish-green jelly with big black eyes.

The squid blinks in the bright spotlights and shudders at the noise from the spectators. The terrified creature yanks its tentacles loose and retreats deep into the water.

Once more it attacks, grabbing Floyd by the leg and trying to drag him under.

"Do it again!" you shout. You and Patty pounce on the squid, hauling it back out of the water.

This time, when it breaks free, it disappears in a cloud of ink.

You win!

Turn to PAGE 110 to celebrate!

You back away from the dark opening. It's way too creepy in there. "On second thought, who needs a prize?" you say quickly. "I'll just take a soda instead."

Silently, the hot-dog man scoops a can out of a cooler and takes your money. He flips open the counter, and you're out of there.

"Didn't you get your prize?" Patty asks.

"I decided it wasn't worth the risk," you reply. You pop open the top of the soda can.

"Huh?" Floyd exclaims, peering at the can in your hand. "I never heard of Ghoulie-Cola before."

You read out the list of ingredients. "Eye of newt, toe of frog . . ."

Swallow hard and turn to PAGE 55.

"Yip! Yip! Yip!"

You whirl around at the sound. The whole mound of hot dogs is moving now. They're all squirming toward you!

Your heart pounds with panic as you watch hundreds of tiny mouths flashing thousands of tiny teeth. "Yip, yip, yip," they squeak.

Gulp! They sound hungry!

"Where's the tent-flap?" you cry. You scratch and tear at the canvas with both hands. But you can't find an opening. It seems to be a solid wall now!

"Ow!" Sharp teeth nip your shins. You hop around in pain, stumbling over more hot dogs. You crash to the ground.

Hungry hot dogs swarm all over you. You try to swat them away. But it's no use. There are too many of them!

You're buried in hot dogs!

You try to scream for help. But a hot-dog bun whizzes out of nowhere, right into your mouth. "Mmmrrmmph!" you cry.

Well, it's only fair. You've gobbled down dozens of dogs. Now for every big bite of a hot dog you've ever taken, these critters will take a little bite out of *you*!

Looks like this time you've really let yourself go to the dogs.

THE END

"Yikes!" you cry. "What do I do now?"

It's dark inside the computer screen. And crowded!

"Yeowch!" you yelp. Something pokes into your back. Your knees are scrunched up around your ears. And whatever you're sitting on is sharp and lumpy.

You pull something out from under you and peer at it.

A letter "W."

You shift around and discover you're sitting on piles of letters.

"Hey!" you cry.

A "T" and "X" land on your head. Whenever you move, more letters crash down around you. You are buried in letters!

What now?

Well, you're good at word puzzles. Can you unscramble this message?

HET NDE

"I bet you thought you were smart, hiding on that farm," Big Al growls. "But we tracked you down. Now you and your friends have a second chance to visit with us . . . forever."

You stare at Big Al. You are too terrified to respond.

"You remember the rules, don't you?" He gives you a mean smile. "You have until midnight to win your freedom. If you win three games or more, you get to challenge me in the grand finale."

"What happens if we lose a game?" Patty asks.

"If you lose any games . . ." Big Al laughs. "Well, if you survive losing, you'll enjoy eternity as one of us!"

Uh-oh! Turn to PAGE 99.

The Roller Ghoster seems like the best idea. You'll be able to see the whole carnival from up there. And maybe you'll spot a way out.

"Hop aboard," the operator says. "Step lively, now!"

Patty goes first, then you, and finally Floyd. The man with the cigar clamps down the safety bar, and you notice something you don't usually see on a roller coaster.

There's a steering wheel in front of you.

"What's this for?" you ask.

"You get to drive this marvelous machine!" the operator explains. "Choose your own route for maximum chills and thrills!"

"Hey!" Patty complains. "*I* want to drive." She starts to shake the safety bar. "Open this up! I want to sit in the middle behind the steering wheel!"

"Too late," the man says. "Here come the rest of the cars."

Turn to PAGE 72.

You and your friends land with a thump in a dark hole.

"Everybody okay?" you ask.

"Yup," Floyd responds.

"Okay enough," Patty answers.

"At least we got off that revolting roller coaster," you say. "Now all we have to do is climb out of here —"

You stop when you hear a strange noise. A soft slithering sound.

"Let's get out of here!" you cry. You reach for a thick rope hanging in the shadows.

But before you can grab it, the rope grabs you!

It's not a rope at all, you realize with horror. It's a twenty-foot python — and it's wrapping itself around you.

A rattlesnake strikes out to bite Floyd, while a cobra attacks Patty. But there's nothing you can do! The python squeezes so tight, you can barely breathe.

Spots dance before your eyes as you think back to the sign you saw. Was part of it broken off?

It must have been.

Because you've wound up in a *Snake* Pit Stop!

THE END

The squirmy sensation under your feet is much stronger now. The vibrations feel as if they are coming right through the soles of your shoes.

Your shoes! The slug slime must be a very strong acid! It's eating away the soles of your shoes!

"We've got to get out of here!" you yell. You take a step.

But the Slug Subway moves in the opposite direction.

You walk forward — but your feet are pulled backwards by the slugs!

You start to run. So do Patty and Floyd.

"Eeeeeeyah!" you howl. Your feet! The slime has eaten all the way through your shoes. Now you feel as if you're running across a sandy beach on a hot day.

A *very* hot day.

You try running even faster, but you slip on the slimy slugs. You fall.

"Yahhhh!" It's like landing in a red-hot frying pan. The slug slime coats your skin, burning it away. You, Patty, and Floyd scream for help. But no one comes to the tunnel.

Oh, well. Better luck next slime!

THE END

No way is Patty bossing you into that killer game. "Forget it," you tell her. "We need a game we can win! Come on."

Patty and Floyd follow you down the midway. You spot a booth decorated with blinking dollar signs. A big computer screen flashes different sayings:

YOU BET YOUR LIFE!

NOTHING VENTURED, NOTHING GAINED!

DOUBLE YOUR MONEY, DOUBLE YOUR FUN!

The little man running the game wears a derby hat and a vest with big gold moneybags on it. He hops around, waving dollar bills.

"I'm Big Buck, test your luck!" he cries.

"How do you play this game?" you ask.

"Easy," the man tells you. "All you have to do is answer that question." He jerks his thumb at the computer screen. It now reads:

ARE 1997 DOLLAR BILLS WORTH MORE THAN 1902 DOLLAR BILLS?

"Huh?" you say. "A dollar is a dollar!"

Floyd digs his elbow into your side.

"Play the game," he murmurs. "You can beat this guy."

Why is Floyd so certain? Find out on PAGE 96.

"You *are* lucky!" a voice shouts.

"You win a prize!" someone else in the crowd cries.

You smile at the game operator, who only scowls back at you. But before you can say anything, you hear a loud, staticky voice shouting over the crowd:

"MAKE-WAY, MAKE-WAY!"

The mob parts, and a strange robot pushes through. Its legs seem almost like human limbs, except that they're made of metal. But the robot has no arms or head. And its body is a big electronic screen. It looks like a walking signboard!

"What's this?" Floyd asks.

"I-AM-YOUR-PRIZE," the robot's voice bleeps.

Patty snorts. "It looks like a giant digital clock," she comments.

"Can you give the time?" you ask the robot. This thing could make a great talking alarm clock!

"PREPARING —" The screen flashes brilliantly several times.

Get the message on PAGE 106.

You wait as Floyd hits more buttons.

Just as the doorknob turns, Floyd jumps up. "Okay. Now!"

You all leap for the glowing Space/Time Door hanging in the air. You tumble through, and land in . . . Big Al's office!

You peer around. Big Al isn't here. *Whew!*

"That didn't get us very far," you grumble.

Floyd darts back to the desk, pointing at a screen. "Far enough. We've gone back a month in time!"

He's right! There's the date on the screen right in front of you. The screen is set up like a calendar, with all kinds of "To Do" lists. Scrolling ahead, you come to the day you went — or will go — to the carnival. Between "Do Laundry" and "Start Diet" is the entry "Get —" Hey! That's *your* name there!

Running back through the computer calendar, you see all of Big Al's plans to take the Carnival of Horrors to Floyd's hometown. "Can you erase all this?" you ask.

"Even better," Floyd assures you. "I can fiddle with these plans so the carnival goes anywhere we want."

A smile creeps across your face. "How about Antarctica?"

Floyd hits some keys. "Done!" he announces.

FWOOOMP! Everything goes black!

Turn to PAGE 74.

The Log Zoom is nearby. Maybe it will be the way out.

Or maybe not.

The three of you hurry to the ride entrance. It's decorated to look like a lumber camp. A three-foot-tall man dressed as a lumberjack gives you a big smile. "Wooden you like a ride?" he asks.

"Boy, you're a real cut-up," you joke back.

"Cut-up? *Cut-up?* Hoo! Hoo! Hoo! I like your sense of humor, kid!" The little lumberjack slaps his knee. "Hop in!" He waves at the nearest log-boat.

You, Patty, and Floyd scramble into the boat. Floyd almost tips over the boat climbing in. Finally, all three of you are settled. You strap yourselves in.

You also check to see where the life preservers are stored. After all, this is the Carnival of Horrors!

You grope around under your seat and feel a life preserver there.

"This might be fun," you say to Patty and Floyd.

Your log starts bobbing as a fresh rush of water fills the ready area.

Here you go! Down the waterfall!

Zoom over to PAGE 66.

"Whoa," you murmur. "Losing is serious business here."

The man running the racing booth smiles at you. You stare at his green skin and big, bulging eyes. He looks like a frog.

"Ready for some smooth moves?" he croaks. "Want to put the pedal to the metal? Do you have the *drive* to play this game?"

"I don't know," you answer. "If I lose, one of those blue tornadoes comes and gets me." You shudder, thinking about the old woman.

"No way!" the froggy man promises. "You have my word."

"Well . . ." You're not sure. You glance at Patty and Floyd. They're depending on you to escape from the carnival. And to do that, you have to keep playing games. "What do you think, guys?"

"Go for it," Patty advises.

That's Patty, all the way — she's up for anything.

But Floyd shakes his head. "Don't do it. I've played that road-race game. It's very, very hard to win."

Who will you listen to? Floyd or Patty?

If you do what Patty suggests, turn to PAGE 44.

If you take Floyd's advice, turn to PAGE 89.

You can't wait a moment longer! Big Al is almost here!

Grabbing Floyd by the shirt, you haul him out from behind the desk. You also seize Patty's hand. "Come on!" you yell, pulling them toward the glowing rectangle.

You twist the doorknob and shove Patty and Floyd through the Space/Time Door. Then you step through yourself.

You stumble on hard-packed dirt. Glaring lights dazzle your eyes. Loud music blares in your ears.

You blink, look around, and realize where you are. There's the Roller Ghoster, and the midway and, in the distance, the Hall of the Mountain King.

Then you glance at your watch.

"Oh, no!" you groan.

You're still in the Carnival of Horrors — you've just gone back to earlier in the evening!

"I knew I didn't have those coordinates fixed quite right," Floyd wails.

You stare wildly around. "Come on!" you order again. "We have to get out of here!"

You've gone back in time. All the way back to PAGE 59.

You twist the wheel to the right. With a shriek of wheels on rails, the Roller Ghoster lurches — and makes the turn!

You shudder at the grisly face hanging in front of you. "You won't stop me!" you shout.

The dead face continues to float in front of you. You glare at it. You won.

So why is the ghost smiling?

With a series of jerks, the Roller Ghoster slows down.

"We must be coming to the pit stop," you tell Patty and Floyd. "The moment we stop, get ready to jump out."

You're barely chugging along. The ghost's face is still laughing into yours, so you can't see what's ahead.

But Patty and Floyd can.

"Look out!" they scream.

"The tracks just end!" Patty shrieks.

The Roller Ghoster stops just as the first car — *your* car — goes over the edge!

Drop down to PAGE 87.

You gaze up at your cousin. "How do you know we can win?" you demand.

"I collect coins," Floyd explains. He bobs up and down with excitement. "Money from 1902 is worth a lot more than modern money."

You watch Big Buck stacking up two big bundles of money. "I don't know," you murmur. "He looks really confident to me." You wonder if there is some kind of trick to the question.

"Trust me!" Floyd sounds totally sure. "I have all these books about money at home. Old paper money is very rare. And anything rare is more valuable. Go on, bet him! Tell him that 1902 dollar bills are worth much more. You'll win."

Your cousin's advice sounds good.

But is he right? Will you win your next game?

If you think Floyd is right, turn to PAGE 56.
If you think Floyd is wrong, turn to PAGE 13.

"I'm going to try it!" you shout, leaping out the escape hatch. You bend your knees and hold out your arms for balance. "Wee-hah!" you whoop. Fake lizard scales zoom beneath your feet. It's like the world's coolest, scariest skateboard run!

Swooping to the end of the dinosaur's tail, you zip over the fence surrounding the Carnival of Horrors.

"HAHAHA!" you laugh in delight. "We did it! We escaped!"

You thump to the ground. A second later there's another thump, then a "WHOOOOOA!" and a crash from Cousin Floyd.

At first, you can't see your friends. A heavy fog steams up from the ground. The air feels a lot warmer than when you arrived at the carnival.

You find Patty, and then Floyd. He's examining a bush and seems very excited. "This is an amazing scientific find!" he cries. "Everyone thinks this plant has been extinct for millions of years."

Before you can answer, the earth starts to tremble. You hear the sound of huge, heavy, stomping feet.

And they're heading your way!

Turn to PAGE 109!

"Do you hear a —" you start to ask. But your question is drowned out as the noise turns into an ear-jangling snarl.

Your eyes slowly adjust to the darkness. You begin to make out something up ahead.

Oh, no! A huge buzz saw hangs in the middle of the shed!

And the awful noise is the sound it makes as it carves its way through the empty log-boat ahead of you!

"We've got to get out of here!" you cry.

Which is the best way?

Should you hop out of the boat immediately?

Or should you try to stop the boat before it reaches the buzz saw?

If you jump out of the boat now, turn to PAGE 41.

If you try to stop the boat, turn to PAGE 32.

Before you can answer him, Big Al vanishes in a puff of smoke.

"Th-this *is* for real!" Floyd gulps. "What do we do?"

"Start playing games," Patty cries. "We only have until midnight!"

"But which games?" you demand. You gaze around.

The booths nearest you have old-fashioned games like a ringtoss and a mechanical claw. "Forget about the ringtoss," you tell your friends. "Those games are always rigged."

You step up to the mechanical claw game. A big plastic claw dangles over a heap of tiny toy people. You recognize this game. If you can fish out one of the toy people with the claw, you get to keep it as your prize.

"Those toys," Patty marvels. "They look so — so real."

You shake your head. "We shouldn't try this one, either. No one ever wins this game."

"Maybe somebody here could tell us what to do," Floyd suggests, waving a hand at the weird, pale carnival people.

Start playing games on PAGE 54.
Ask for advice on PAGE 114.

100

"Route One!" you cry triumphantly. "It even spells a message. 'An Easy Way Out Is Good.'"

The man behind the counter laughs nastily. "An easy way out *is* good — for us! But it's not the *shortest* way out!"

He presses a button, and the maze vanishes from the computer screen. A picture of a giant pair of warty lips appears. They pucker up, as if they're going to whistle. But, no! Instead they suck in a steady stream of air.

A powerful wind pulls at you. It gets stronger and stronger. You feel as if you're caught in a hurricane.

"Help!" you cry to your friends. But your voice is drowned out by the howling gale. You grab on to the counter of the booth as you're pulled off your feet.

SWOOSH!

You're sucked into the screen!

Turn to PAGE 84.

"Whoa!" you gasp. You're so astonished, you drop the lantern.

You bend over, staring at the runaway hot dog. "Yowch!" you cry. You feel a sharp pain just below the hem of your shorts. You peer down.

One end of a hot dog sticks to your leg. Its body waves wildly. You reach down and yank it off.

It leaves a bite mark the size of a dime on your leg!

Holding up the attack-wiener, you see that it has a little mouth — and hundreds and hundreds of little teeth.

The mouth opens. It doesn't say "Yip!"

It says, "Yum!"

Turn to PAGE 83.

102

Big Al grins at you. "Lucky Day is one of my favorites," he booms. "That's because the guy who runs it is one of my favorite helpers." He pushes you, Patty, and Floyd up to the booth. "Meet Horrible Hairy Harry!"

Horrible Hairy Harry certainly lives up to his name. He looks like a cross between a gorilla and a troll. All he wears is a pair of Bermuda shorts. The rest of him — even his face — is covered with thick brown greasy-looking hair.

And he's nine feet tall!

Yikes!

You wonder whether there's still time to change your mind. "Uh, I —" you begin, turning to Big Al.

But there's no sign of the carnival manager. He's gone!

Instead, a crowd of the creepy carnival people closes in behind you.

"Play! Play!" the crowd chants.

Big white teeth appear in the fur on Horrible Hairy Harry's face. You figure that's a smile.

"Is today your Lucky Day?" he growls.

Listen carefully to the rules on PAGE 112.

The little flashlight flickers out. You grope around and grab the knob on the door that's marked WAY OUT. "We haven't had much luck on the rides," you declare. "I'll give this a try."

You twist the knob and heave the door open.

Uh-oh. It's just as dark on the other side. And Patty's flashlight is all used up!

You take a tiny step forward. A strange force whirls you right through the doorway!

You shiver in the freezing cold surrounding you. You're floating in darkness, surrounded by diamond-bright pinpoints of light that look like stars.

In fact — they *are* stars!

And isn't that a meteor whizzing by? And off in the distance — gulp — Earth!

The door was a way out of the Carnival of Horrors, all right. Way, *way* out — to the ends of the solar system. And way out of this adventure!

THE END

104

With the lights in your eyes, you can barely make out the spectators in their seats. They look more or less human. Some seem to have too many arms or an extra head. But they're all clapping.

"Hu-mans, hu-mans, they're okay! Hu-mans, hu-mans, hip-hooray!" half the crowd cheers.

The other half yells, "Go, squid!"

"At least some of them are on our side," Floyd offers hopefully.

The unseen announcer keeps talking. "Taken together, the challengers weigh in at around two hundred twenty-five pounds. They have chosen the small size of opponent."

So the guy in the boat listened to your request. You're up against the small squid.

This doesn't sound so bad.

Does it?

Go to PAGE 33.

The signboard robot clanks over to stand by Big Al.

"What are we going to do?" Patty asks, gazing at the photo in terror.

"Simple," you answer in a low voice. "We make sure Big Al doesn't play against *you*." Then you call to the carnival manager, "I'm ready for the final challenge!"

"Fine," Big Al replies. "I'll just pick the game —"

"Why should you?" you interrupt. "I think *I* should choose."

"Oh, no," the carnival manager disagrees. "According to the rules on your ticket . . ."

"What ticket?" you demand. "I never got a ticket."

"No?" Big Al cries, shocked. "Quick! Print them a ticket, Igor."

The signboard robot clicks and whirrs. A ticket large enough to be a poster pops out of its top.

"According to clause three of paragraph eight," Big Al begins.

You grab for the gigantic ticket. "Let me see — YOWTCH!"

The ticket flies from your hand as you dance around in agony. The edges on that ticket are as sharp as razor blades!

Floyd reaches to catch the fluttering cardboard. "DON'T!" you yell.

Turn to PAGE 7.

106

A series of numbers appears on the robot's body. They look like this:

01:00:00:03
01:00:00:02
01:00:00:01
01:00:00:00
00:59:59:59

The number in the far-right column reels down incredibly quickly.

You stare at the weird numbers, trying to make sense of them.

Floyd points at the robot's screen. "Those must be the hours," he says, indicating the numbers in the left-hand column.

"So the next ones are the minutes," you say, catching on. "And the ones after that are seconds, and then fractions of a second."

Patty lets out a low whistle. "That's exact!"

"Yeah, but it still doesn't tell us the time, exactly," you argue. You watch numbers fly by in the seconds column on the display. "What kind of clock is this?" you ask.

Don't waste time! Turn to PAGE 37.

No way can the Roller Ghoster jump over that gap. And you can't stop the cars from careening into space. You've got a steering wheel, but no brakes!

You're doomed! Unless . . .

Okay, you tell yourself. You may not be able to keep the coaster from crashing. But you might be able to get yourself and your friends out alive!

You wait till the Roller Ghoster is level with the top of the castle walls. Then you jam the wheel to the right, *against* the curve. With a loud squealing of wheels, the cars almost come to a stop. Your heart pounds.

"Everybody out!" you yell to Patty and Floyd. "Everybody alive, that is!"

And then you leap!

Turn to PAGE 31.

108

You step in front of the screen.

"Is the kid a winner?" the game operator shouts. "Watch and see!"

People gather behind you to watch you play. Colored lights appear on the screen and spin around.

Whoa! They're making you dizzy! You clutch the counter.

The screen goes foggy. It clears into a maze of letters:

"The shortest message is the quickest way out. Find it, starting . . . now!" the man cries.

Is Route 1 the shortest? Turn to PAGE 100.
Or is it Route 2? Turn to PAGE 22.

"M-maybe it's the mechanical Tyrannosaurus rex from the carnival," Patty suggests. Her voice shakes.

"R-right. It probably broke through the fence," Floyd agrees. You notice beads of sweat on his face.

You strain your ears. The footsteps seem to come faster than the speed of the Dino-Ride. And it sounds like they're coming from another direction. . . .

"I have a feeling we did go back in time," you say. "But not just a night or two."

A head bursts out of the fog, and you scream.

It's a Tyrannosaurus rex — but it's not the one from the carnival. The colors are all different — and this creature's eyes aren't portholes. They peer down at you with a greedy, hungry expression.

"RUN!" you yell.

But before you can move, the Tyrannosaurus rex bends down, gripping you in its teeth.

Wow! You really did go back in time — millions and millions of years *back*!

This sure does beat watching a dinosaur movie — except for one small problem. . . .

You're the snack!

THE END

110

Dripping wet, you haul yourself back onto dry land. Then you help your friends out of the water.

"This is my favorite white T-shirt," Patty complains. "Now it's got squid ink all over it!"

"Patty! I think we have bigger things to worry about," you scold. "We don't have much time left before we're trapped here forever!"

"Hey!" Floyd calls. "I found the exit."

You race through the door and bump into a pale woman with shadowy eyes. She wears a red sequined dress. A feather boa is wrapped around her neck. Her lipstick and eyeshadow are the only colors on her face.

You shudder. If you don't get moving, you'll become a prisoner of the carnival, just like this woman!

You notice she carries an armful of towels. Maybe she'll let you use them. And maybe she can give you advice on how to escape from the Carnival of Horrors!

Turn to PAGE 115.

You duck your head down. "Come on," you whisper. "Just try to blend in." You take a few steps — but the others aren't following.

You turn back to Floyd. His eyes are wide, and his mouth hangs open.

"Snap out of it!" you whisper. "We've got to move fast if we're going to keep Big Al from finding us!"

"Look!" Your cousin's voice trembles as he nods toward the midway.

You glance in the direction he is staring. You freeze too. Now you know why Floyd was so freaked out.

Big Al has disappeared from the screens. Now every single monitor shows you, Patty, and Floyd.

The people in old-fashioned clothing begin to mutter and murmur around you. Some stare at you. Some point. Others step away, as if they don't want to be anywhere near you, just in case . . .

Just in case what? you wonder. You shake your head.

Don't even think about it, you tell yourself. Just get out of here — fast!

Hurry to PAGE 73.

112

"The game is easy," the huge, hairy creature behind the counter promises. "You don't have to do a thing — I'll take care of it all. Now you see, certain days are lucky, and certain days are unlucky. It all has to do with birthdays. I've made a special study of them over the years —"

"He should have studied hair care instead," Patty whispers to you.

Horrible Hairy Harry keeps talking. "You tell me your birthday, and I'll tell you if today is your lucky day. It depends on whether your birth date is an odd or an even number."

Horrible Hairy Harry leans right over to you. "So, which is it?"

Your heart beats faster as you tell Horrible Hairy Harry your birthday.

If your birth date is even, like February 18, April 6, or November 30, turn to PAGE 119.

If your birth date is odd, like January 9, June 13, or October 31, turn to PAGE 90.

"Wait! We're not wrestlers!" you yell. "Really! We never signed up or anything!"

"Yeah," Patty joins in. "I don't even like cala-mari!"

"Good luck!" the boatman calls over his shoulder.

A barred gate rises out of the water to pen you in. You're trapped in what seems to be an underwater boxing ring.

"You have to wrestle your weight in squid to get out of here," the boatman yells back at you. "Luckily, we have a squid that weighs as much as all three of you put together!"

He rows out of sight around a bend in the river.

Brilliant lights come on, spotlighting you and your friends. The water is up to your armpits. You peer down into the murky water and notice something moving.

"What's that?" you mutter.

THWAP!

You get your answer. A thick, slimy tentacle lashes through the water. It coils around your chest. And squeezes!

Turn to PAGE 69.

"I think we need help," you say. You search the midway for a friendly face. But all you see are blank eyes in pale, waxy skin.

A man wearing cowboy clothes bumps into you. His wide-brimmed hat falls to the ground.

"E-excuse me," you stammer as you pick up his hat and hand it to him. "Could you tell —"

"Mighty chilly for this time of year," the man cuts in. His eyes seem to stare right through you.

"For October?" you ask, surprised.

"It's August," the man insists.

What's with this cowboy? you wonder. He seems to be a few acres short of a ranch! You clear your throat. "I'm sorry, mister, but it really is October."

"I know what day it is!" the man snaps. "I've been looking forward to today for weeks. I circled it on my calendar. The day the carnival comes to town. August 3, 1872."

You hear Patty and Floyd gasp behind you. "W-what year did you say?" you sputter.

"It's 1872, young 'un. Don't you know anything?"

You stare at the cowboy. Has he really been a prisoner of the Carnival of Horrors for more than a hundred years?

Go to PAGE 34.

"Can we use some of those towels, ma'am?" you ask.

"Call me Pia," she answers in a hollow voice.

She gives you some towels. She doesn't seem too weird. For a carnival creature, that is. Maybe she'll help you.

"Uh, Pia," you say. "What we really need is a way out of here."

"Who doesn't?" she replies. "I tried to beat Big Al at the games on the midway." She nods toward the brightly lit booths. "They'll let you go if you win — but I lost. I've been here ever since. Who knows?" she adds. "Maybe you'll have better luck."

Then the woman turns her haunted eyes toward the rides. "I've heard stories that there's a way out somewhere over there."

You follow the woman's gaze to a sign that reads DINO-*SAUR* BACK IN TIME ON OUR DINO-RIDE!

"Back in time!" Patty cries. "That sounds like just the ride we need. It'll make up for some of the time we lost!"

"Let's get on it," you say. "It's almost midnight!"

Should you try the midway games? Turn to PAGE 54.

Should you give the Dino-Ride a try? Turn to PAGE 117.

You slap a hand to your forehead. How could you have forgotten the elves? They were part of the ride to the Hall of the Mountain King.

The terrifying part!

Last summer, you thought the ride would be fun. Everyone climbed into cute little wooden donkey-carts to ride up to the castle.

But the elves spoiled the fun by using their axes to chop up the carts.

And then they chopped off people's heads!

Now the elves are marching toward you, swinging their sharp, shiny axes.

"Run!" you scream to Patty and Floyd. You dash back up the trail to the castle.

The elves follow. "Heads!" they cry. "Chop off their heads!"

"Hurry!" you pant. "Hurry!" You dart around the bend. You race toward the castle.

Oh, no! The castle gate! It's closed! And enormous chains are padlocked across the front. There's no way in!

You turn to face the elves.

Bad idea. They may be little guys . . .

But they're also a big pain in the neck!

THE END

The Right Away Railroad sent time spinning forward. Maybe the Dino-Ride will move time backwards!

You hand Pia the wet towels. Your shoes squelch, but you're a lot drier now. You head for the Dino-Ride.

"Cool!" Floyd exclaims.

"Awesome!" Patty agrees.

You gaze up, up, up at the Dino-Ride. Passengers ride on giant mechanical dinosaurs — or rather, *inside* them. A Tyrannosaurus rex stands bent over, its head to the ground. Its mouth full of big, sharp teeth hangs wide open. Where a tongue ought to be, there are four padded seats with safety belts.

"This will be fun to ride even if it doesn't help us escape!" Floyd declares.

You climb over the fangs and settle into a seat. "We need to win back some of our time," you worry. "It's getting closer and closer to midnight. If we don't find a way out soon, we'll be trapped here forever!"

Stop wasting time and turn to PAGE 35.

118

"Hold on," you burst out. "Do you think we're stupid? I remember the last time we were here. You and your creepy pals chased us all over the place! Why should I trust you now?"

"Big Al *ordered* us to chase you," Ernie argues. "We had no choice."

"Then he could make you trick us again," you reply.

"Yeah," Patty chimes in. "For all we know, he could have told you to come and talk to us right now."

For a second, Ernie looks sad. Then he becomes furious. "You should have trusted me," he growls. "Now you'll never get out of this place alive!"

Turn to PAGE 134.

Horrible Hairy Harry shakes his head. "Oh, how sad!" he mourns. "Today is a *very* unlucky day for you." He's so upset, he starts crying.

"Oh, please!" Patty exclaims. "Just get it over with! What's going to happen to us?"

"Your terrible luck means" — Harry takes a deep breath — "that you have to leave this wonderful carnival!"

"What?" you gasp.

"I know, it's terrible," he wails. "Poor you."

Horrible Hairy Harry blows his nose on his fur. Gross.

"Um, yeah, it's sad, really sad," you babble.

"I'm so sorry I have to do this." Harry pulls aside a curtain behind his booth. It opens onto the carnival parking lot.

"Forgive me, kids," he sobs, and pushes you through.

"We'll forgive you eventually," you say, trying not to grin with happiness. "We just need time to get over it."

"I'll tell you what," Harry says. "Take these." He hands you three cardboard strips, then closes the curtain.

"Thanks," you call after him. Then you glance at the cardboard strips in your hand.

Oh, no! Guess what Harry gave you?

Free passes to the Carnival of Horrors!

THE END

You close your eyes as you tumble through the air. Then you hit the ground with enough force to knock the air out of you.

If you weren't in such a hurry, now would be a good time to collapse.

But it's almost midnight. And you still have to find the ride that will help you escape the Carnival of Horrors!

"We're closest to the Log Zoom and the Roller Ghoster." You turn to Floyd. "Do either of those sound like time-travel rides?"

Floyd shrugs. "I don't know," he admits. "What do you think, Patty?"

"We'll be able to see the whole carnival from the Roller Ghoster," she declares. "I vote we take that!"

"No, let's go for the Log Zoom," Floyd argues. "It might *zoom* us out of here!"

You wonder if Floyd really means that. Or is he just sick of being bossed around by Patty?

Anyway, it looks as if the final decision is up to you.

If you want to try the Roller Ghoster, turn to PAGE 14.

If you decide on the Log Zoom, turn to PAGE 92.

It's dark and shadowy inside the sawmill. "Ow!" you mutter after you bang your shins on a large piece of metal.

The sawmill seems to be a junk warehouse for the Carnival of Horrors.

"Hey!" Patty's excited voice echoes across the room.

You trip and stumble over to where she's standing.

"I found a door," she reports.

Groping in the dark, you feel the doorknob.

"There's some kind of sign attached to the door," Patty explains. "You can feel it."

Floyd trips his way to you. "Too bad we can't read it."

"Wait!" Patty cries, digging into her pocket. "I have one of those key chains with a built-in flashlight. I hope the battery isn't dead." She pulls out her key chain and gives the tiny flashlight a pinch. A dim beam of light shoots out.

The sign on the door reads WAY OUT.

"All right!" you cheer. "We're history!"

Take the WAY OUT on PAGE 103.

"Let's head for the rides," you decide. "I think it might be easier to escape from one of those than from the midway!"

You can feel Floyd trembling as he clings to you. He walks so close, you trip over his big feet. Patty takes the lead. As usual.

The people around you wear old-fashioned clothes. A nearby girl holds up her long skirts with gloved hands. A man with a handlebar mustache tips his straw hat as you pass.

They are Big Al's prisoners — and assistants. Stuck in the clothing they wore the day the carnival came to their town.

"Attention! Attention!" a voice booms.

You recognize that voice. That's Big Al, the horrible manager of this vile carnival.

You glance back at the midway. And gasp!

The Wheel of Fortune has stopped spinning. The rifle games have stopped popping. And all of the computer games are projecting something horrible on their screens — Big Al's face!

And he's staring straight at you!

"No use trying to get away." His voice echoes out of every speaker in the carnival. "We are going to get you!"

Yikes! Turn to PAGE 111.

You grab Floyd and Patty by the arms. "Come on!" you yell. "Behind the booths!"

You notice that there's a narrow open space — an alleyway — behind the booths. You figure it's a path for the carnival workers.

The three of you stumble along the shadowy passageway. Old candy wrappers and paper cups litter the ground. The only light comes from a strange green beam that shoots down from a weird-looking machine behind one of the booths.

As you hurry through the green light, a roar goes up from the crowd behind you.

"There they go!" someone shrieks.

"Perfect. Big Al will be pleased with us!" another shouts.

That doesn't sound good!

"Come *on*!" you gasp, tugging at your friends.

Then Floyd lets out a horrified yell.

"L-l-look!" he shrieks, pointing upward.

Take a peek on PAGE 17.

"Do what Patty did!" you yell to Floyd. "Tie their tentacles together!"

Your cousin's face is blue, and his eyes bulge, but he tries to follow your advice.

You grab a tentacle from one of the squid on your legs and try to tie it to a tentacle from the one on your arm. The stringy, boneless tentacles squirm, trying to break loose as you knot them together. You yank hard, and — POP! the creature on your arm comes off.

Turn to PAGE 9.

"Let's search the castle!" you decide.

"Okay. But where should we start?" Patty asks.

You gaze up at the castle towering above you. "Let's go to that tower and then climb to the top," you decide. "We can work our way down."

You take a twisting outside staircase of stone to the base of the tower. You walk around it until you find the door.

Locked.

"Look!" Patty cries.

You rush over. She's pointing at the gargoyles and other strange carvings that decorate the outside of the tower. If a person was careful — or desperate enough — they could climb the carvings to a window in the tower!

Before you can protest, Patty starts climbing.

You and Floyd scramble after her.

"This is pretty tough," Floyd grunts, pulling himself up.

"Yeah," Patty agrees, clinging to a gargoyle's nose. "The only thing worse would be to have something attack us up here."

You hear the flutter of wings.

Uh-oh.

Turn to PAGE 25.

"Hey!" you shout. The wind over your head gets stronger and stronger. You raise a hand, trying to fan the wind away.

Instead, your hand is caught! It feels as if your fingers have been sucked into a vacuum cleaner.

"Yeeeoooow!" you yell. The wind tears at your wrist. You pull, heave, and swing your arm around. But you can't break loose of the wind. You glare at the frog-faced man.

"I thought you said no blue tornado!" you cry.

"Hey, I kept my promise!" The man's bulging eyes sparkle gleefully. "Take a look."

"Aaaaaghh!" you scream. The tornado of light swallows up your shoulder. Now you know why the old lady shrieked. It feels as if your body is being stripped away a spoonful at a time.

But the frog-faced guy didn't break his promise.

You aren't being eaten up by a blue tornado. You're being eaten up by a *purple* one.

THE END

"Okay," you announce. "I won three games. And we have the camera." You take a deep breath. "I think it's time to challenge Big Al."

"All right!" Patty cheers. "Let's beat him!"

You, Patty, and Floyd go back to the tent where you met the ghoul-boy in the knickers. He's still lurking in the shadows.

As you walk up, he darts out and grabs your wrist with an icy hand.

"Did you get it?" he demands in a whisper. His face looks even paler than you remember. "Do you have the camera?"

Answer him on PAGE 11.

128

"Wow!" you exclaim, stepping into the weighing room. It's huge! Much bigger than the booth looked from outside.

The vast room is dark, except for the glowing silver disk set into the floor. You cross the enormous space and step on it.

A faint mist rises all around you. A computer-like voice says, "Measured. Guess your weight."

Okay. Find out what you weigh, down to the half-ounce. Now, multiply that by 2.19. This is Figure A. Next, measure your height — in centimeters — and divide that by 3.6. This is Figure B. Multiply Figure B by Figure A. Carry the six ... add it to — wait, no — *divide* by two ... then multiply it by the number of jumping jacks you can do in ten minutes ...

Hey! This is supposed to be a *fun* book!

What's with the math lesson?

There is a less technical method you can use: *Guess.*

If you guess that you weigh about two and one-half times more on Jupiter than on Earth, turn to PAGE 58.

If you guess that you weigh about two and one-half times less, turn to PAGE 43.

Holding the lantern in front of you, you squeeze through the flap. You find yourself in another tent. Piles of hot dogs and mounds of buns lie on the ground. This must be some kind of storeroom for the hot-dog booth, you guess.

"Yuck," you mutter. "And Mom thinks *I'm* messy!"

You hold your lantern higher, peering into the corners of the tent.

No Charlie. And no prizes.

As you pass a pile of hot dogs, you step on one. *"Yip!"* it cries. Then — like a giant caterpillar — it crawls away from you!

Turn to PAGE 101.

"I can't believe I missed!" you yell in disgust.

You thought you'd lined up the points perfectly. But with one eye closed, you couldn't tell what's near and what's far. The dagger points did not meet.

"I'm so sorry." But the young woman doesn't look sorry. In fact, she seems a lot less friendly now. Her rotten fangs flash again as she gives you an evil smile. "You'll have to pay the price of losing. And keep paying — forever!"

"No way!" You clutch the daggers in your hands. "My friends and I are definitely leaving this carnival!"

You whirl around, and the crowd shrinks back. They know you mean business!

Maybe this is what you should have done from the beginning — *fought* Big Al and his carnival creeps.

March right on to PAGE 36.

Jump out of a moving train into unknown, pitch-black water?

No way!

You may be desperate, but you're not stupid!

The train chugs even more slowly over the bridge. And your watch seems to spin faster! Minutes pass like seconds, hours like minutes.

This train's name turns out to be horribly on target. The Right Away Railroad is taking your precious time *right away*!

And you're helpless! All you can do is sit and shiver.

At last! You see a shoreline up ahead.

"There's dry land!" you yell. "And there are some other rides! Let's jump out! On your mark, get set . . ."

GO! To PAGE 120.

"Hey!" you call. "Yeah, you," you add as the kid tries to slink deeper into the shadows. You, Patty, and Floyd dash over to him.

"You're going to get me in trouble," the kid whines.

"We want to see Big Al," you say. "I'm tired of playing against the clock. We want to go straight to the grand finale!"

The boy looks shocked — and a little scared. "Are you sure that's a good idea?" he squeaks. "Big Al always cheats, you know."

"I'd rather go up against the main guy himself," you declare. "It beats getting zapped in one of these crazy little games."

Even *you* are surprised by how confident you sound.

Because inside you're shaking harder than a bowl of jelly on a bicycle.

Jiggle over to PAGE 38.

You decide to trust Ernie. You stroll over to the Hand-Eye Challenge.

Big Al lets out a sinister laugh and disappears in a puff of brown smoke.

"This looks like a good game," you declare. You have good coordination. Maybe the game will be something like juggling.

"I don't know," Floyd says doubtfully. "I never do well at that kind of stuff."

"That's why we're not asking *you* to play," Patty tells him, snickering.

A pretty young woman sits behind the counter of the booth. A green silk eye patch covers her right eye. She seems almost normal. Friendly, even.

Then the young woman smiles at you — revealing big yellowish-brown fangs.

You jump back, startled.

As long as you're jumping, leap to PAGE 26.

You watch Ernie stomp off. He approaches clusters of carnival people on the midway. Every time he stops and talks, they all stare at you.

You wonder what he's telling them. "Maybe we should get out of here," you suggest.

"Yeah," Floyd agrees. "They look kind of mad at us."

Trying to act casual, you, Patty, and Floyd stroll down the midway. A low rumble comes from the crowd behind you. Then somebody yells, "Get them! We'll bring them to Big Al!"

You and your friends pick up speed. The carnival people surge after you.

"Run!" Patty shouts.

"Which way?" Floyd cries.

You glance around frantically. "There are some big games up ahead," you pant. "We'll find a place to hide over there."

"What if these guys catch us first? I say we try to lose them behind the game booths," Patty argues. She points over at the row of booths with the claw game and the ringtoss.

You look back. The mob is gaining on you!

What do you do?

If you run full speed ahead, turn to PAGE 62.
If you dash behind the booths, turn to PAGE 123.

The old woman winks at you. "Well, hop aboard."

Shuddering a little, you step onto the carpet of slugs. They feel sort of icky under your feet. Once you have both feet firmly planted, you start to glide along.

Wild!

"Come on, guys," you call to Patty and Floyd. "This is weird, but it's kind of cool!"

They join you on the trip down the tunnel. It feels almost like surfing — except for the odd squirming sensation under your feet.

When you reach the halfway point, Floyd starts sniffing the air. "What's that funny smell? It's like burning rubber."

You smell it too. Then you notice smoke coming from your cousin's feet.

"Is there something wrong with your sneakers?" you ask.

"If there is, we all have the same problem." Floyd points to you and Patty.

You gasp.

Smoke is rising from all your shoes!

Uh-oh! Get to the bottom of this on PAGE 88.

"I will now point to the symbol you landed on," the blindfolded woman declares. She removes her hood.

You gasp. She has three eyes.

She reaches out her long, thin hand and taps a symbol:

"How did you know?" the Civil War soldier demands.

"I know all," the woman answers. "Including the fact that you lose!"

Before the soldier can reply — he explodes!

The smoke clears. The soldier has vanished.

And the woman is now staring straight at you. With all three eyes.

"Would you like to play the game?" she asks. "Do you feel lucky?"

You glance at Patty and Floyd. They both shrug.

Time is running out. Decide!

If you want to play Q Quest, turn to PAGE 23.

If you decide to forget the games and head for the rides, turn to PAGE 122.

You stop walking and snap your fingers. "Hey, I've won three games!" you declare. "Isn't it time for the final challenge?"

"Yeah!" Patty exclaims. "Where's Big Al?"

"Did somebody call my name?" a deep voice rumbles.

You jump and spin around. Big Al is right behind you! How does he *do* that?

The carnival manager isn't wearing his checkered jacket. His black mustache is rolled up in two enormous curlers.

"Who wants me? I was about to take a nap," he growls.

Squaring your shoulders, you step up to him. "You said if I won three games I could take the final challenge," you state. "Well, I won three games."

Big Al glares at you. Then his frown changes to a nasty smile. "Did I say three games?" he purrs. "I meant *four*."

"No fair!" Floyd yells. "You can't change the rules!"

Big Al throws back his head and laughs. "Kid, you're a riot. Don't you know I can do anything I want?"

He points to a booth with a crowd around it. A neon sign over the front flashes LUCKY DAY! LUCKY DAY!

"If you want to take the final challenge," he declares, "you'll have to try your luck first."

Step up to the booth on PAGE 102.

About R.L. Stine

R.L. Stine is the most popular author in America. He is the creator of the *Goosebumps, Give Yourself Goosebumps, Fear Street,* and *Ghosts of Fear Street* series, among other popular books. He has written more than 100 scary novels for kids. Bob lives in New York City with his wife, Jane, teenage son, Matt, and dog, Nadine.